Allan McFadden trained as a secondary school music teacher and has worked as a teacher, music arranger, actor and theatre composer. His scores include: *Madame de*; *Noli me Tangere*; *Air Heart* and *My 60's Hero*. As an author he has written the stand-alone novels *Big Gig in Rock 'n' Roll Heaven* and *Sumbar on Sumbeach,* along with the Dougay Roberre series, beginning with *Au Revoir, Mate!* All books are published by Austin Macauley.

For my French mates:

Cedric Perolini
and
Andre Mollard

Allan McFadden

ELLE EST MORTE, MATE!
(SHE IS DEAD, MATE!)

AUSTIN MACAULEY PUBLISHERS™

LONDON • CAMBRIDGE • NEW YORK • SHARJAH

A CIP catalogue record for this title is available from the British Library.

ISBN 9781035871629 (Paperback)
ISBN 9781035871636 (ePub e-book)

www.austinmacauley.com

First Published 2024
Austin Macauley Publishers Ltd®
1 Canada Square
Canary Wharf
London
E14 5AA

The Dougay Roberre series:
Book One: *Au Revoir, Mate!*
Book Two: *A Bientot, Mate!*
Book Three: *Une Autre Fois, Mate!*
Book Four: *Nous Nous Reverrons, Mate!*
Book Five: *Elle est Morte, Mate!*

Notes

All characters and situations in *Elle est Morte, Mate*! are fictional. They bear no resemblance to anyone alive or dead.

The areas and streets of Nice, Athens, Samos, Kusadasi, the ancient sites of Turkey, Gallipoli Peninsula and Arles exist, though what happens there is fiction.

Maman (French) means 'mother'.

Ne c'est pas (French) means 'Does it not?'

RSL: Returned Services League (Australian): a national organisation of licensed social clubs.

Neh (Greek) means 'yes'.

Hotel Samos exists.

Hosgeldiniz (Turkish) means 'welcome'.

Tusan Hotel, south of Canakkale, exists.

Stairway to Heaven is a song written by Robert Plant and Jimmy Page.

Young love, first love, filled with true devotion is a lyric from the song *Young Love* written by Ric Cartey and Carole Joyner.

Tall and tanned and young and lovely is the opening lyric to the song *The Girl from Ipanema*. Music: Antonio Carlos Jobim. Original Lyrics: Vinicius de Maraes. English Lyric: Norman Gimbel.

Take Me Home, Country Roads is a song written by Bill Danoff Taffy and John Denver.

Crazy, crazy for feeling so wealthy is a corruption of the lyric of the song *Crazy* written by Willie Nelson.

You walk by and I fall to pieces is a lyric from the song *I Fall to Pieces* written by Harlan Howard and Hank Cochran.

I've Got Your Records and She's Got You is a variation on the lyric of the song *She's Got You* written by Hank Cochran.

Hit the Road, Jack is a song written by Percy Mayfield.

On the Road Again is a song written by Willie Nelson.

Ca va? (French) means 'How's it going?'

Skerrick (Australian) means 'the smallest bit'.

Merde (French) means 'shit'.

François Couperin (1668-1733) was a French composer.

Mate (Australian) is a term for a friend, though it can be used ironically.

Chapter 1

The Cannes Film Festival had come and gone. Actress Belinda Swann had not made an official appearance, though keeping her head down she had witnessed, along with art patron Antoinette St Romaine, my friends and me, the screening of *Au Revoir, Mate!*

This was the final film of her late husband, star actor Calvin deMarko. It had been screened only once in an out-of-the-way cinema, out of competition, late one Sunday evening. The film had become too hot to handle because its producer, Harold Kempenski, was in custody in America awaiting trial, charged with having had sexual intercourse with underage teenage girls in exchange for featured roles in his movies.

His pet project—a double movie adaptation of the two classic *Heidi* books— was now, after two failed attempts, never going to see the projector's light, the life well and truly sucked out of that Swiss Miss.

Because of Kempenski's scandalous behaviour, my special friend, Mary-Anne Walton, who worked for Kempenski as his personal production assistant, stepped off the stern of the *Blue Dahlia*, a motor yacht moored in Cannes. The boat was returning from a bay over near the Italian border where I'd once spent an unforgettable weekend in her embrace.

Mary-Anne's body was never found—the Mediterranean is wide and deep. In the USA, charges had been laid against her—for *The Procurement of Minors for Sexual Exploitation*. I guess that's the equivalent of being accused of being a modern-day slave trader.

I know she hadn't procured underage girls for Kempenski because I'd heard honest stories from those who'd experienced Kempenski's roaming hands, and they'd never implicated Mary-Anne. The media and the overly concerned, righteous citizens of the world had been braying for blood, and the blood they'd brayed for had been hers. Sadly, Mary-Anne had had enough.

How had I become so obliquely entangled in all of this?

I'd started out as a go-between for Mary-Anne and the Oscar-nominated screenwriter Philip J Phillips, delivering to her aboard the *Blue Dahlia*, the work in progress of the screenplay for *Au Revoir, Mate!* I'd even given Phillips the final line of his script, which became the film's title!

Next, I'd worked for Kempenski as a second unit director, supervising a film shoot of Swiss mountain tops, not to mention being responsible for the starlet who'd been cast and the starlet's mother! The fifteen-year-old *Heidi's* confession at a televised press conference had been the KO punch which had splattered Kempenski around the ring.

Since Mary-Anne's disappearance, I've not been my usual self. That kick in the guts hasn't healed. It's a constant reminder of happier days, though we really only spent three or four in each other's company. I guess the ache comes from a lack of satisfaction. You see, I'd been planning an endless summer with her, and all I ended up with was an auditory memory of a doleful twangy electric guitar plucking some tune called: *It Was Never To Be*.

Understanding the impact on me, Madame Legrande, the lovely old lady who lives on the ground floor of my apartment block, suggested I get away, to go where Australians go. I thought she meant London. Rather, she meant Gallipoli, over in Türkiye.

"You need to take your mind off things, dear."

Like my business partner, Claude Tanguay, co-owner of *L'Opera Mozart*, I said, "I'll think about it."

*

My best mate, Remy Didion, owned a warehouse containing used furniture, *bric a brac* and high-quality junk in the *Le Piol* area, near the Russian cathedral *Saint-Nicholas a Nice*. He'd been a professional boxer, and most Saturdays, I sparred with him to keep fit. I'd been taught to box back in Australia by a friend of my father, and Remy was always amazed that I didn't hold my hands the wrong way, or try to fight standing on my head, or hop about like a kangaroo! Remy has a 'special' brand of humour.

Lately, I hadn't been in the mood to throw a punch at him; however, this Saturday afternoon, with a spring in my step, I headed up Avenue Auber, along Avenue Thiers, right into Boulevard Gambetta and under the railway line to his warehouse. I banged on his metal roller door and as usual, he opened the single solid steel one.

"Keep it down," he said, "you'll wake the *Sleeping Beauty* I have upstairs."

"The only *Sleeping Beauty* you have in that gloomy mezzanine of yours is the child's book left behind in a chest of drawers, some down-and-out mother has had to sell, to allow her family to eat this week. You haven't on-sold my brand new kitchen, have you?"

"Not yet, though I'm considering it, as your storage fee wasn't paid again this month."

"My storage fee is the price I pay for tolerating your dubious humour!"

We put on sparring gloves and did more dancing and weaving around each other than exchanging pulled blows. Still, at the end of twenty-five minutes, we were both gasping for air and sweating like pigs.

"You're getting out of condition," I said. "You're lucky I've decided to come back and wallop your ass!"

"Like this?" He quickly retorted and made to thump me there.

Ready for his tricks, I jumped away and his fist swiped air. I skipped about imitating his perception of a boxing kangaroo, poking out my tongue.

Glaring back, he falsely admonished, "You're so childish!"

We washed off in the large sink, which not only took care of our sweat but also used turps, dead beer, flat cola, squashed coffee beans and unidentifiable stain-making liquids. Upstairs Remy made coffee; downstairs we sat and sipped it.

Remy studied me over the rim of his chipped coffee cup. "What's this I hear about you going to Arabia?"

"Not Arabia, Türkiye. And how did you know?" I was surprised he'd asked, as I hadn't yet made up my mind.

Remy merely tapped the side of his nose. "I know everything," he bragged.

"Well then, if that's the case, what team won the Australian Rules Football Grand Final in 2005?"

He twisted his lower lip, thinking. "I know everything except that."

I thanked him for the coffee and asked if he'd be able to manage by himself with the washing up. As I approached the roller door, he tripped me from behind. I fell forward into it. The loud crash was drowned out by his laughter.

*

I was walking home beneath the railway underpass when I saw a most peculiar thing.

A young woman, in her twenties, was slowly pushing an older woman in a wheelchair on the other side of the road. As the wheelchair entered the darkness of the underpass, a young man, also in his twenties, walked towards them. As they passed, the young woman turned her head to him, and he turned to her, and they kissed! He kept walking and she kept pushing the wheelchair. The woman in the chair had no idea what had happened behind her back.

How odd, I thought as I walked out into the sunlight and turned left towards the railway station and home. *Still, there's nothing odd about snatched moments of young love, Dougay!*

*

Sitting in Place Mozart, adjacent to my apartment building, I was once again whiling away a late Sunday morning, listening to Madame Legrande reminisce on her favourite topic—a time and a France long gone.

"Ah, Bardot," she said. "As a young woman, she was so beautiful, so teasingly innocent, so alluring."

I'd never seen any of her films, though I managed to recall a magazine photograph of her I'd once seen in a Sydney dentist's waiting room. I remembered at the time being impressed.

"As a child," she went on, "I once saw Bardot on the sand at St Tropez. Well, I hardly saw her, as she was surrounded by a gaggle of sycophantic photographers." She paused a moment, savouring the memory. "Beauty attracts all sorts and not usually the types you'd like attracted—users, sexual rovers, false-hearted lovers."

"I'll never leave you, Madame," I consoled.

She turned and took my eye. "Dougay, I do not know if I should be thankful or fearful." She suddenly turned her head, instinctively sensing something. "Look! Here's Pierre."

Pierre Legrande, her elder son is a 'businessman'. He operates a service called *Milady*, which hires out classily trained and beautifully groomed call girls, replete with a petite *fleur de lis* tattooed on their buttocks.

"Dougay," he said, respectfully nodding his greeting.

"Pierre," I said, nodding likewise.

"*Maman*," Pierre said to his mother, kissing her on both cheeks. "Time I walked you inside, as you don't wish to catch sun-stroke out here."

"What about Dougay catching sun-stroke?" She asked, cheekily, knowing full well that her son wanted a word with me in private.

"Who cares if Dougay burns or not?" He asked as cheekily as his mother had.

He escorted her carefully from the park across Avenue Auber to our apartment block. I looked about for Big Luigi, Pierre's bodyguard. He was trying to look inconspicuous, hiding in a sliver of shade under a pinkish-red blossomed tree.

I gave him a wave, calling out loudly, "*Bonjour*, Luigi!"

He was not pleased. I'd exposed him to whoever he believed he was hiding from. I smiled, knowing he was feeling uncomfortable, his 'cover' blown.

I had an odd relationship with Pierre Legrande and his younger brother Raphael, who worked on the other side of the fence to his brother. Raphael was a police detective. Soon after I'd purchased my apartment here, I'd saved their mother's life. I now know that it was the most important thing I'd done since arriving in France. She'd had a heart attack—on the very bench I was sitting— and I'd immediately called for the ambulance and rode with her to the hospital. The brothers had never forgotten. Therefore, I had the ability to be available for them, and they allowed me to have access to them; an access I'm sure most others in Nice only dreamt of, or feared for.

Pierre returned and took his mother's place on the bench next to me. "*Maman* tells me you're going to Türkiye."

How many others have been reading my mail? "No, well, so far she's suggested it, and I've only said I'll think about it."

"Think about it harder," he said, taking a business card from his wallet. "You may like to book your tickets and accommodation through these people. I highly recommend them."

I read the card. *Eastern Mediterranean Tours.* I looked at him, knowingly. "You wouldn't happen to own this company, would you?"

"Not outright," he admitted. "There's no need for concern. They are independent, though I do own twenty percent. Rather like you with that famous cafe around the corner."

The cafe he referred to was, of course, *L'Opera Mozart*. Its fame resulted from my organising a three-painting exhibition there a few months back in the spring—*Mozi-Art 1.0*—and the national notoriety of two of its paintings.

"I have no say in the running of *Eastern Mediterranean Tours*," said Pierre, "though I can get for you a ten per cent discount."

Pierre Legrande never, ever, said at the beginning of a conversation what his real intentions were. Madame Legrande had told me it was a trait both of her sons had picked up from their father.

"So, Pierre, I do not believe you've come over here to personally recommend to me a travel agent. What is it you really wish to ask?"

He laughed. "Dougay, I'd like you to accompany me to Zurich—overnight. We fly in, you accompany me to a bank; you can swim in the hotel pool; we dine at a vibrant restaurant I know; we get a good night's sleep; we have breakfast and we fly home."

"Luigi can't go?"

"Luigi goes with me wherever I go, *ne c'est pas*? People expect that of him. If I leave him here to wander about, then no one will suspect I've left town."

That made sense. "When?" I asked. "When would you like to go?"

"I'll be in touch. Go to the travel agent." He indicated the card he'd given me. "Introduce yourself to Madame Cartier and leave her your passport details. She's expecting you."

"Okay."

"Türkiye," reflected Pierre. "The land of shish kebabs with yoghurt, tomato salads, cold beer, freshly baked pita bread, ancient ruins, rocks and sand, and desperate widows charging down the gangways of cruise ships, itching to get their hands on a prospective husband!" He leant forward and slapped me on the upper leg. "What isn't there in Türkiye for you to enjoy?"

Chapter 2

At *L'Opera Mozart*, Claude was sitting at a table in the back room, in through the archway. He rarely sat there and certainly not with a morning coffee in his hands, staring at it.

"Claude, is everything okay?" I asked, concerned.

He looked up as if he hadn't recognised my voice. "Oh, Dougay!" Sitting up straighter, he gathered himself. "Yes, I'm okay. I've had sad news this morning."

I gathered that he'd finally heard on the slow-moving grapevine that his ex-lover Marcel Valiquette had died, a year back in a plane crash on Galaban Mountain outside Aubagne. So I pulled out the chair opposite and sitting, waited for him to explain. Claude surprised me. The news he'd received wasn't about Marcel.

"My old football coach has passed away," he said, tapping the side of his large coffee cup as if trying to call up his spirit from the other side. "Daniel Artaud. What a leader! What a teacher! What a man! Why does the loss of some people far outweigh the loss of others?"

I thought the question was rhetorical. It wasn't. Claude looked at me as if I held the answer.

"Time of your life," I offered. "The impact he had on you as a teacher and mentor, kindness, an understanding of the developing male?"

"Ball and all, Claude! Ball and all!" he stated forcefully. He then smiled affectionately at the memory. "That still rings inside me after all these years."

"He coached you at rugby?"

"Yes, rugby is popular here in France."

I didn't tell him I knew that. Instead, I asked, "Another coffee?"

"Sure. Are you having one?"

"In my café, the coffee is free!" I said, trying to bring a smile to his face.

"Only twenty per cent of the cup is free!" answered Claude, beginning to smile. He was going to be okay. I left him to his thoughts and went off to make the coffee. Returning, I placed the two cups before us.

"When's the service?"

"Two days. *Notre Dame.*"

"Mmm. He must have been famous."

Claude stared back at me, my ignorance dawning on him. "No. The service will be held at *Notre Dame de l'Assomption*—in Nice." He laughed. "Not *Notre Dame* in Paris."

*

I wore my quality dark suit. At *L'Opera Mozart*, Louise Modisette, our chef, waitress and my flatmate, was clearing away an outside table. She stopped when she caught sight of me walking towards her. She attempted a sexist wolf-whistle. Young women can be so disrespectful!

"It's a solemn occasion, Louise, please show some dignity."

"The words 'dignity' and 'Dougay' are never uttered in the same sentence." She laughed and headed inside. Stopping, she turned and said seriously, "Claude's been waiting for you for the past thirty minutes."

I looked at my wristwatch. "I'm not late."

"No, he's anxious." She came to me and planted a kiss on my cheek. "You look lovely, papa!" She hurried off laughing before I could fake a bum-slap!

Claude and I walked to *Notre Dame de l'Assomption* along Avenue Georges Clemenceau. At the tram line, we turned left. Well-dressed people were now joining us, Claude stopping to offer and receive condolences. We moved intermittently forward in an unorganised procession. A woman in front of me, crossing Avenue Jean Médecin, caught her high heels in the tram track. As she stumbled forward, I caught her before she fell. She apologised and thanked me.

Claude asked facetiously, "Does every woman in France fall for you?"

I smiled; pleased again that he wasn't suffering his old football coach's loss so much that he couldn't offer me a humorous *bon mot*. He took me by the arm, and we joined the large crowd in front of and below the cathedral's façade, dominated by the neo-gothic circular grill and twin towers.

"Dougay, I did not expect you to be here," commented Old Hector, one of the regular customers from the café.

"I'm here for Claude," I explained. "Give him my support."

"Good soul." Old Hector paused. "Both—you and him. Dougay, I'd like to introduce my brother to you. He was a star half-back under Coach Artaud. This is Louis Laurent."

"Pleased to meet you, Louis." I offered my hand.

He took it. "Likewise. I hear so much about the Australian who has revolutionised my brother's favourite café."

"Hardly revolutionised."

Jules St Croix, the private detective I'd done dubious jobs for, shuffled over. He didn't have his camera around his neck, for which I'm sure everyone was thankful.

"Louis Laurent!" he exclaimed. The two men hugged. "If I remember correctly, Hector told me you were onto your fourth wife."

"Sadly, that has ended."

"That's too bad," consoled Jules.

"Not really. I admit I'm a slow learner, but I've now learnt from my mistakes," said Louis philosophically. "The next beautiful woman I meet, I'm simply going to buy her an apartment. Cut out five years of heartache."

We all laughed and then realised we were at a funeral!

A hand took my shoulder from behind. "What are you doing here?" It was Remy. "You've only ever thrown forward passes."

"No passes at you, that's for sure."

With Remy was Serge, an old friend of his, a caretaker of a building, the basement of which is used to shoot films of a dubious nature. We'd met several times, and I had invited him to share Christmas lunch with all my friends at *L'Opera Mozart*.

Standing, listening in the small group of old friends, I soon learnt that this bunch had all been to the same school and had played at various times in the same rugby side together.

"We were comrades in arms," stated Louis.

"You may not believe this, Dougay," said Claude, "but we were champions."

"Yes, the old days, gone now," commented Serge sadly.

"Remember when Remy came to the game in dirty white shorts?" Claude prompted, igniting memories. They all did, nodding as the thought returned. *"Standards, Remy. In my team, there will be standards.* Coach Artaud told him to take them off, take them home, and wash them in the sink with detergent so they'd be clean for next week."

"Yes. Though he gave me another pair to wear!" insisted Remy. "Contrary to the myth generated by you memory-addled lot, I did not score a try wearing only my mud-stained underpants!"

"So, at home, Remy washes the shorts," continued Claude, explaining for my benefit, "not in detergent, but mistakenly in starch! Next week he turns up and he can't run. His shorts are too stiff!" They all laughed at the memory.

I followed them solemnly inside, the dark of the cathedral swallowing us.

The eulogy of a life well-lived, well-loved and well-respected, was given by the coach's grandson. My mind drifted to the funeral of Avril Goumas, the last I'd attended, and from her to the murdered Danielle Hubert and of course, to the lost Mary-Anne Walton. Will I always be haunted by the memory of these women? I hoped the faces would remain at three because I didn't want any more ghostly females crowding in there.

Seventy minutes later, we all filed past the Artaud family on the steps of the cathedral offering our condolences. All the old rugby players stood with the family and conversed while I waited off to the side. I sniffed. There was an odd smell in the air.

The grandson took Remy aside, and in a huddle, they spoke. I took a few steps forward, trying to work out where the smell could be coming from.

When Remy joined me, I asked, "What did the grandson want?"

"My autograph." I don't think Remy was joking. "What's that smell?" He asked, deliberately looking at me.

"I don't know."

Remy walked to the bottom of the steps and looked skyward. The others joined him. We were all now looking over the top of the cathedral.

"What is it?" I asked.

"Car tyres," said Old Hector, pointing. "Smoke like that could only be coming from car tyres."

From behind the cathedral rose a long column of thick black smoke. There was no breeze in the air so the column rose directly up as if the cathedral was offering Coach Artaud a direct line to heaven.

"Burning car tyres is environmentally unsound," said Claude.

"I agree," said Old Hector.

"Old habits die hard for some people," commented Serge, disapprovingly.

"I hope the culprit managed to toss in the petrol can and run away before it all exploded," said Jules. "There's nothing worse than singed eyebrows." We all looked at him, for he'd implied he had first-hand experience of the act. Seeing our faces, he exclaimed, "Not that I'd know!"

*

M'sieur Pom is the elderly caretaker of my apartment building. He lives with his wife in the apartment immediately behind the desk he occupies in the foyer, along from and opposite to the one owned by Madame Legrande. He's always quoting from the newspaper, or the television, keeping me up to date with what's going on in Nice. He loves 'who's who' and 'what's what'—though he's not a simple gossip. I guess he's a social historian; he's just never written any of the stuff down. He was the one who first told me, inadvertently, that Mary-Anne Walton had gone missing from a boat near the Italian border.

"Things are sure heating up in the back blocks of Nice!" he called out as I closed the elevator's door.

"What's heating up?"

"There was a fire over in *Vallon des Fleurs*."

"Anyone injured?"

"No."

"That's good."

"Not for the car yard owners." I waited for him to explain; I knew he would. "A used car lot has gone up in flames. *Automobiles des Qualité*. That's a grand name for a used car yard."

"Was the fire an accident?"

"Ace reporter Mimi Benoit doesn't say. It's probably too early to know."

"So they managed to extinguish the fire?" I asked.

"Yes, of course!"

They may have literally extinguished the fire; however, knowing fires can have drastic consequences, I doubted they'd extinguished it metaphorically.

Chapter 3

Locking the front door of *L'Opera Mozart*, I headed home in the twilight with Louise. She put her key into the front door of our apartment block, and I pushed against it letting her slide past. M'sieur Pom had toddled off to bed, the light from beneath Madame Legrande's apartment was out, and the elevator, of course, was not waiting for us.

I indicated that we should climb the stairs. Louise shook her head and quietly said, "Patience, Dougay." The elevator eventually arrived.

On the sixth floor, as I opened the door to our attic apartment, I asked, "Hungry? Feel like *Spicey-Ricey*?"

"I *am* hungry and I do *not* feel like *Spicey-Ricey*!" Louise hates my attempts at Asian cuisine. "I'll whip up an omelette instead."

"Great! That's exactly what I had wanted you to say."

I set our small dining table, placing a knife and fork for each of us on touristy Riviera plastic placemats, facing each other.

Breaking eggs into a bowl, Louise asked, "When do I get my new kitchen?"

"*Your* new kitchen?"

She ignored my correction of ownership. "When can you start?"

"Soon, Louise, soon."

"Dougay, you're becoming as vague as Claude."

"Oh, alright, tomorrow," I stated, without really thinking. "Is that soon enough for you? I'll visit Remy in the morning and borrow his tools."

"Thank you, papa!"

I turned on the television, explaining to Louise, "There was a fire yesterday over near the cathedral where the funeral of Claude's old football coach was held. I just want to see if there are any further developments."

A distraught man sat in the gutter, head in his hands. A name at the bottom of the screen read: *Marcel Valleaux, proprietor.*

From outside, the police taped off a cordon around the used car yard and a reporter addressed the screen. *Yesterday's fire in the western suburb of Nice, Vallon des Fleurs, is now officially an arson investigation.* An image of the sign over the building, *Automobiles des Qualité* flashed onto the screen.

Detective Raphael Legrande was interviewed. *Anyone knowing anything about this heinous act is asked to call us. Any piece of information, any suspicious behaviour around the car yard, anything—please call.* Clearly, the cops had no clue.

The distraught man from the gutter was interviewed, a microphone unceremoniously thrust beneath his chin. *My brother and I are honest law-abiding citizens.* A shot showed several cars gutted by flames. *I know of no one who would want to do this. This act of bastardry has ruined us.* The camera panned around the gutted showroom, all the walls smoke-damaged and beyond repair. *My brother and I are effectively wiped out!* Smouldering burnt-out tyres were shown stacked in the far corner. *Our business will never recover.*

"Aren't tyres usually stacked outside in a garage or shed around the back from the main building?" Louise asked, dividing the contents of the frying pan in two and shovelling the equal portions onto our plates. "Who stacks car tyres inside, in a corner of a car showroom?"

I carried the plates to the dining table, answering, "Someone who wants to set the whole business alight. Someone who wants to destroy two brothers!"

We sat and began to hungrily eat.

Louise thought about that and put down her fork. "Or someone planning on making an insurance claim."

"I don't think so. Not in this case. Look at the owner. I can't see anything false about his reaction. He's as devastated as his business."

"The other brother must be in a bad way," Louise commented. "He can't even be interviewed or sit with his brother for moral support."

*

"Arson!" declared M'sieur Pom as I crossed the foyer heading over to Remy's to begin my kitchen installation. "That used car yard was the work of an arsonist!"

"Yes, I saw it on the late news last night."

"Who do you think did it?" He asked.

"Me? How would I know?"

"You have contacts. That private investigator pal of yours, for instance."

"Jules? He doesn't know the name of his own mother!"

M'sieur Pom laughed. "Talk to Raphael Legrande."

"M'sieur Pom, you're going to have to be satisfied with finding out about it in the newspaper. I have a new kitchen to install and I can't be wasting my time enquiring after matters to satisfy your insatiable desire to know everything that's going on in Nice."

"Back in Australia, did you disappoint your friends as much as you do here?"

I laughed. "Good morning, M'sieur Pom. Have a great day." I started to leave.

He called out after me. "If I wait for the cops to find out, I'll die of old age!"

*

"I have nothing on for the day," said Remy. "I'll come over and give you a helping hand."

I couldn't believe what I was hearing! I feigned a heart attack, clutching at my chest, reaching out to a chair for balance.

Remy studied me. "What a pity, the nominations for best actor at Cannes this year have already closed."

I smiled and seriously said, "Remy, it's going to take more than one day. What do you have on tomorrow?"

"Nothing. Well, nothing of importance, other than helping a second-rate tradesman install a first-rate kitchen."

Remy followed me over to where my kitchen cupboards and appliances were stacked. They were still boxed in their cardboard casings, which meant he had not poked his head inside for a sneak preview. We carried them and placed them at the rear of his truck.

"Come on, lift!" We began to heave them up. Once loaded, I struggled, lifting into the truck Remy's heavy toolboxes.

"Any chance you might help me?" I asked, straining.

"Are you hiring or borrowing my tools?"

"Borrowing!"

"Hiring includes assistance; borrowing doesn't."

Laughing at his poor humour, Remy climbed into his truck. "Come on! What are you waiting for?" He asked.

"A decent gag!"

"Let's go! Time's money! Get in!" I did. "Your problem, Dougay, is that you have such high conversational standards." He laughed again and back-handed me on my upper thigh!

Remy's truck sprang into life and he drove us over to Avenue Auber where he parked illegally on the footpath out front.

"I suppose you want me to make a contribution towards the petrol," I said slyly.

"Not today, I'm feeling generous."

M'sieur Pom met us at the front door. "Go around the back. I don't want you ruining my marble floor!"

"When we get there, can you carry something for us, M'sieur Pom?" I asked.

"No. But I will hold open the rear door for you. Someone has to stand back and supervise."

Remy relocated his truck down the back alley and we managed to get all the stuff up to my apartment after a number of elevator rides. On the fifth pass by the fourth floor, descending, we stopped. Old Monsieur Degas climbed in.

"Ah, Dougay, I heard you were installing a new kitchen. I thought you were going to Türkiye."

Everyone in the building knows my business!

*

Remy and I attacked my existing kitchen cupboards with a crowbar and hammer, and at the end of the afternoon, we carted all the broken pieces and the old stove downstairs to his truck. Once it was dark outside, we revisited the illegal dumps around town Remy had introduced me to when I first arrived here and had renovated my bathroom.

"The key to illegal dumping," instructed Remy, "is to spread the load. Dump portions in several places. That way busy-bodies don't notice the piles as much and don't complain to the Council."

After Remy had dropped me off back home, I lay on the lounge room floor and stretched my back, groaning, trying to rid myself of stiffness, aches and pains. Louise walked in from the café.

"I thought you had a woman in here!"

"Very funny!"

I tried getting up. It wasn't going to be easy. I rolled onto my belly and pushed up. My arms ached too much to hold my weight. I gave up and rolled over onto my back again.

"Where's the stove gone?" Louise asked, surprised. "There's no stove in here."

"That's what happens when you put in a new kitchen. You've got to toss out the old."

"What are we eating for dinner tonight?"

I hadn't thought of that. In my haste to begin the renovation, I hadn't even set up an electric fry pan to compensate.

"There's money in my wallet," I told her. "Go get two pizzas. I'll just remain here on the floor!"

For the next two days, Remy and I toiled and on the evening of the third, under the bright glow of the kitchen light, I turned on my new induction cooktop with my new specially designed pot. I heated water.

"Wow!" exclaimed Louise. "Look how fast it came to the boil!"

*

In the morning, earlier than usual, I was swimming my half hour, when on the first lap, turning at the airport end of my designated area, I again recalled the flashing lights down there and the body of Avril Goumas being lifted from the water. Trying to put that thought to one side, I thrashed harder on the second lap.

Having completed my swim, I stood with the towel around me, the sun climbing out of the sea behind, soaking up the calm morning's light and offshore breeze.

"This sure feels like paradise!" I addressed out loud to no one in particular.

A young couple, up on the promenade, were discussing something, their hands gesticulating. He tried to kiss her, I guess reassuring her that everything would be okay. *Probably planning their future together,* I thought, the romantic in me coming to the fore. Then the realist kicked in. *She's having second thoughts.*

He walked away from her, changed his mind and turned back. It was the young man from the underpass and she was the young woman who'd been pushing the lady in the wheelchair.

By the time I'd completely dried myself, pulled on my clothing, gathered up my towel, stumbled across the stones, and climbed the steps, they'd gone.

Walking back to Avenue Auber, my phone rang. It was Francine. "Dougay, are you free today?" Before I could offer a salacious reply, she added, "I need your help. I'll pay you; however, it has to be today."

"Of course, Francine. Are you home?"

"No, I'm at the office."

"I've been swimming so let me walk home, change and have breakfast. I'll be over there about nine. Is that okay?"

"No, come as you are," she said with urgency in her voice. "I'll send out for a croissant when you arrive."

*

Francine Delange is my lawyer. She is also the woman with whom I've had an on-again, off-again relationship. I fell in love with Francine soon after the night of our first encounter. She didn't like that, as she didn't want any real affection getting in the way of a Friday night fling. She'd kept me away for a while, though I guess my sheer animalistic magnetism drew her back into my arms. Either that or I am so soft-willed I can never resist her offer. Truthfully, it's the latter.

Since then, I've resisted falling in love with her again. It's very difficult maintaining a heartfelt distance when a beautiful, intelligent, older woman removes her reading glasses, unties her jet-black hair, and lets it fall in slow motion down past her shoulders, all the while fixing you with a twinkling glint in her teasing eye. Francine possesses many self-contradictions and she has social aspirations which I can never fulfil. She is engaged to the gay mayor of Nice.

To a lot of people, that type of relationship sounds crazy. It doesn't to me. She calls me when she needs to vent her frustrations, and as I said, I'm there for her. Sometimes I'm there before she's even hit the red icon on her mobile terminating the call!

Francine Delange's law office is near *Gare de Nice Riquier*, the train station before the tunnel heading east to *Villefranche-sur Mer*. I took a cab to Rue Beaumont, rode the elevator to the third floor of her building and stepped out, automatically turning left. I opened the outer door to Francine's office and stopped.

The secretary's office was a mess! Everything that could possibly be knocked onto the floor had been. The only thing undisturbed was the large office water bottle. The young woman was sitting in her chair, off to the side of her desk, dumbfounded. She'd been crying.

"Are you okay?" I asked, going to her, stepping over a table lamp and strewn papers, putting my arm onto her shoulder.

She looked up. "Yes, I'm okay," she managed to reply. She didn't look it.

"What's happened here?" I called out to the silhouette of Francine in the inner office, attempting to tidy up her desk.

"We've had a break-in," she called back to me.

Francine's office was similar to the secretary's. Every file she possessed was scattered on the floor.

"I need your help, Dougay." She then whispered, "You're the only one I can trust."

Without any further explanation, Francine went to her secretary and handed her some euros. "Go downstairs, sit a while, have a coffee, get yourself together, and bring back a croissant for Dougay."

"Two," I corrected. "Swimming makes me hungry."

The kid nodded she would and dried her eyes on a tissue Francine handed her. As she left, I righted a chair and indicated that Francine should sit.

"You're going to need a new lock on the outside door, Francine. You're lucky the door jam is made of metal and not timber, so there's probably no need to replace that."

"I've already arranged for that to happen. A man will drop by this afternoon at about four."

"Okay, that's good. So, you're employing me to clean up?"

"Not that simple. I need to know which files, if any, were taken. It means finding what's in that strewn mess on the floor and returning it to the correct folder. You'll be perusing my business dealings. As I said, I only trust you, Dougay, to cast an eye over things, return them to their correct file, move on to the next and forget all the details contained within."

"I understand; however, you need not be concerned with my honesty or lack thereof, because I don't read French and I certainly don't read French legalise."

Francine laughed. "I'd forgotten!"

"Don't lose that laugh. You're going to need it before the day is out."

Francine moved to her filing cabinet and pulled open the top drawer. "We'll start with 'A'."

"Francine, why do you still have things filed in a cabinet? I thought everything these days would be stored on a computer."

She hesitated as if weighing up whether to fabricate a story or to tell me honestly. The lawyer in her was struggling with the human being.

"I feel computer signatures are open to fraud, and some of my clients don't trust computers. They insist I retain the old methods regarding their papers. Computers can be too easily hacked."

"And offices can be too easily broken into and ransacked."

"The irony is not lost on me, Dougay. Come on, let's begin."

Francine stood and lifted a clump of papers from the floor. As she placed them on her desk to sort through, I asked, "What were they looking for, Francine? Any ideas?"

"Even if I knew, Dougay, I wouldn't tell you."

"I thought you trusted me."

"I do. I wouldn't tell you because the less you know about things, the better, and the safer for you if anything should come from this."

"Come from *this*?" I asked, indicating the mess around us.

"You have to be absolutely quiet about this break-in. No one must know. People talk. Even months from now, you never know what can slip out during an idle conversation. Some clients are jumpy and very, very concerned about their private business. Silence will protect me." She saw the look on my face. "That's all I'm prepared to say. I trust you, now it's your turn to trust me."

We set about the arduous task of matching clumps of paper with the folder they belonged to. After forty minutes of sorting, I asked, surprised, "*Mascati twins*? You have a file here on the Mascati twins?"

"If that's what it says, then I do." Francine was now sounding well and truly like a lawyer.

"A simple *yes* would have sufficed."

"Dougay, you're in the wrong type of office to get a straightforward reply."

Dismissing my concern, she reached for the small bundle of Mascati papers, shoved them into the folder and placed the folder back into the filing cabinet under *M*.

The Mascati twins are Italian 'businessmen' whom I'd come across when they tried to steal back money from Francine in Milan. I also believed, though I had no proof that they'd supplied Marcel, Claude's ex-lover, with the cocaine that had been found in the plane crash which claimed his life. What was Francine doing with a file on *them*?

Don't ask, Dougay. You said you'd trust her, so trust her.

The secretary returned with my two croissants and Francine told her to take the rest of the day off. The kid high-tailed it out. Francine made coffee and we sat in the outer office on the visitor's chairs, papers still at our feet. I bent to pick some up.

"Leave that," said Francine. "There's nothing of immediate concern held out here in this office."

I ate, drinking coffee with Francine who asked rhetorically, "Who did this?" She bent and picked up a file at random. "There're so many files, like this one, scattered and still bound by paper clips. They've not been read. I get the impression there was a specific file the thief was looking for."

After fifteen minutes, we began again. I stooped and picked up a folder from underneath her desk as if it had been deliberately tossed there to be hidden from view.

"What's this folder?" I asked. "*CIH-D'AZ*? That's a weird name."

"It's a file regarding a partnership agreement between some notable people here on the Cote d'Azur. Have you come across anything that should go into it?"

"Nothing yet."

"Put it to one side. Perhaps…" Francine didn't go on.

We continued searching, collating and replacing the material in the large upright metal cabinet. After about two hours of sorting, the *CIH-D'AZ* folder sat forlornly empty on Francine's desk.

"I guess this is what they were searching for," I said, tapping the *CIH-D'AZ* folder.

"I feared as much."

"Care to explain?"

"Not really."

Chapter 4

It was Monday afternoon and I was clearing away the lunchtime crockery from a table on the footpath outside *L'Opera Mozart*. My last customers, two sunburnt Scandinavians were wandering off, holding onto each other as they stumbled across the street, having over imbibed. After ten metres, they stopped and decided their hotel room was in the opposite direction.

With no one else in the café, I told Louise to finish in the kitchen and take off the remainder of the afternoon. Like Francine's secretary, she didn't stay to argue.

I was wiping down an outside table when a young man stumbled towards me. He wasn't drunk. I'd seen far too many drunks to know that an overindulgence of alcohol wasn't his problem. No, he'd been assaulted because he was carrying his guts as if they were going to fall out of his shirt onto the footpath in front of him. I knew him. He didn't know me; however, I recognised him as the young man from the underpass.

Helping him sit, I said, "Breathe deeply, mate." When he did, I added, "Stay there, I'll get you some water. Don't go off dancing, okay?"

He looked at me as if I was an idiot. What should I have said? *I sure hope your spleen isn't damaged and you won't be pissing blood for the next three days?*

He was still breathing deeply when I returned with a glass of water. I held it to his lips as he sipped.

Louise walked to me from the direction of our apartment.

"What are you doing back here?" I asked, surprised by her reappearance.

"I forgot my key," she said. Taking in the young man, she whispered, "I leave you alone for five minutes and trouble falls into your lap."

"When did you become my mother?" I quipped.

She merely laughed and went into the café. When she returned, the young man was breathing easier though perspiration was now pouring from him. I guess he'd staggered, half-running quite a distance to get away from his attacker. Louise waved me goodbye.

I waved back and returned my attention to the young man. "Want to tell me what happened?"

"No," he managed.

"Ah, well, at least you haven't had the honesty knocked out of you, along with the stuffing."

He studied me, probably trying to assess what kind of Samaritan I was. After consideration, he managed a grunt and a nod of thanks.

"That's better," I said. "You'll soon be healed. This water is mighty powerful; it mends broken bones."

He took the glass from me and drank again. We sat for a while, saying nothing. Sighing deeply, he stretched his torso in the chair, head back.

Back inside the café, I found a handful of paper serviettes and brought them out to him, indicating his forehead. He wiped his face dry.

Eventually, I asked, "What's your name?"

"Is that necessary?" He asked guardedly.

"No. It's just that I don't want to call you: *Bashed Victim Number Seven*."

He nodded, accepting my logic, and smiled. At last, he was appreciating my warped sense of humour. If only I could bottle that appreciation and pass it around for my friends to drink.

"Guy—Guy Franc."

"Want to tell me what happened, Guy?"

"Not particularly."

"Fair enough," I said. "I'll get some more serviettes. You've blood beginning to trickle from your nose."

Instinctively, he wiped his nose, spreading the blood across his face. Again I went inside. I returned with more paper serviettes and carefully wiped his cheeks and nose. When I'd finished, I placed my left hand under his chin and gently turned his face from side to side, checking I'd wiped away all the blood.

"You're very kind, Monsieur."

"It's nothing. You needed assistance."

"Still…" He studied me a moment longer, weighing up what to say further. Then feeling as if he could trust me, he seemed to make a monumental decision. He asked, "Monsieur, have you ever been in love?"

"That's one hell of a question to ask in France," I commented, laughing.

"Ah, what the hell, I may as well tell you. There's this girl," he started.

I thought *there always is!*

"This girl, Cecily, is beautiful."

Aren't they all?

"And she has this brother…"

"And he doesn't want you hanging around his sister, and so he's beaten you up."

Guy stared back at me, not believing. "How did you know?"

"I've experienced a lot of things in life," I admitted, off-handedly.

"She's not the first woman I've been involved with. But I know Cecily is the one. I want to marry her. I have a job. In fact, I've asked her to run away with me."

So that's what they'd been discussing on the promenade!

"Before you advise against it, I've already planned where we'll go." I nodded and waited for him to go on. He dabbed his forehead with the serviette. "I work in a bank and they've given me a transfer to Montpellier. I start Monday week."

"The brother won't let her go?" I asked, filling in the dots, a habit of mine.

"Yes and no. Cecily wants to come, but her mother is dying and she wants to wait here until, you know, she's passed away and there's a funeral. I can understand that. I don't want her to go with me against her will, not before her mother is buried. Cecily would never forgive me."

So, the woman in the wheelchair was her mother and that stolen kiss was probably the only way the two could engage in any form of intimate embrace. However, snatched kisses are no basis for a sustained romance.

That small amount of conversation had exhausted Guy. He slumped back into the chair. I returned inside and brought out a refilled glass of water. He swallowed half of it in one gulp.

"Gunther. The brother is called Gunther. Gunther Valleaux. He went ballistic earlier when we were talking about it. I thought he was going to kill me. I managed to stumble away. It's hard to run holding onto a bashed stomach." I knew exactly what he was talking about.

"Do you fear for Cecily's safety?" I was now concerned, not just for the young man.

"No. He'd never hurt her, only those who want to take her away from him."

Sometimes one has to make a start to right a wrong, or in this case to help young lovers. "What's Cecily's address, Guy?"

Guy Franc looked at me unbelievingly. "You're a waiter. What are you intending to do?"

"Take her brother a coffee."

*

I was in bed, hoping to nod off, having dropped by my side the French children's book I'd been trying to read, when out of the dark Louise called to me, "That man! I've seen him about."

"The young man who'd been assaulted?"

"Yes. I've been lying here trying to remember." I waited for her to go on. There was only silence.

"Do you need prompting?" I called back. "Word associations?"

A moment later she exclaimed, "Got it! He was staying at the hostel, the one I was at before I came here. He was more down and out than I was."

"He's not down and out. He works in a bank. Maybe he'd just been transferred into town and hadn't organised his own place. When I first came to Nice from Sydney, I stayed in a hostel for weeks. It doesn't necessarily mean you're down and out."

"Yes, you're right. I don't remember him being there long because you came into my life and took me away from all that poverty and degradation."

Was she serious?

Louise laughed out loud and clapped her hands with delight, calling out, "Louise one! Dougay nil!"

*

Francine rang.

"How can I help you, Francine?" I asked, concerned. "Not more trouble with your files?"

"No, nothing like that, Dougay."

"I'm pleased to hear that."

"Can you be over here in my office, seven days from now, at 2 p.m.? I don't wish to discuss this matter over the phone."

"Sure," I replied, "I'll be there."

She hung up. I figured she wanted to tell me she'd decided on a date for her wedding and out of courtesy, she wanted to let me know face-to-face before it was splattered all over the local paper.

As if I'm interested in *that* announcement!

*

Thursday morning before dawn, I stood on the footpath outside Place Mozart. A nondescript dark car turned into Rue Beethoven. For me, that's an ominous sign. In the past, dark cars turning into Rue Beethoven have deposited trouble onto my doorstep. This car didn't. Once it stopped, its trunk lifted automatically. I dropped in my overnight bag and sat in the passenger seat.

"*Bonjour*," I said to Pierre Legrande.

"*Bonjour*," he replied.

Nothing else was said as he drove to the airport and left the vehicle in the car park. It was well before our flight, though we still checked in our baggage and went through to the departure terminal. We sat in a far corner, Pierre positioning us so we had a wide view of all those entering.

After twenty minutes, once Pierre had ascertained that we weren't being followed, he asked, "What would you like for breakfast?"

"I'll come with you. I can't make up my mind."

We both stood and walked off. Six steps later, he tapped me on my arm and pointed back to the seat I'd been sitting on. My hand luggage was there on the floor.

"You're too trusting for your own good, Dougay."

"Sorry. I'm still asleep."

I sheepishly retrieved my bag. Over breakfast, I asked Pierre why we were sitting inside the terminal so early.

"We've left France and we haven't arrived in Switzerland. So for these few hours, we're nowhere—somewhere between the two. Who would possibly look for us here in *In-Between-Land*?"

It seemed a bit paranoid to me, but then again, I wasn't the one who needed to go to a Swiss bank. I was thankful I had enough in my bank in Nice though I was reminded I sometimes needed Remy to escort me there when depositing or withdrawing the occasional large amount. I guess I too possess a level of paranoia.

We took a taxi from Zurich Airport to a hotel overlooking the Limmat River. Pierre checked in under the name of Yves Dardonne. He showed the desk manager his passport as proof of identity. I quickly forgot about that detail!

Outside his hotel room door, Pierre said, "Meet me here in twenty minutes and wear that suit I told you to bring."

I opened my hotel room. There was no delectable Russian blonde, secretly working for some unnamed international spy agency, seductively lying on the bed and waiting for my arrival. *How disappointing. Pierre hasn't thought of everything!*

Twenty minutes later, as requested, I knocked on Pierre's door.

"I almost didn't recognise you," he said, as we walked to the elevator.

"This is the real me. I wear that old goat herder's jacket to divert the gaze of beautiful women."

"It's successful."

We took a taxi to a bank on the ground floor of an impressively grand stone building which overlooked the river. Once inside, we were ushered into an office, and Pierre sat opposite an attractive, well-groomed woman who knew he was coming. She was most courteous, full of smiles, and I got the distinct impression she'd dealt with Monsieur Yves Dardonne before. On the desk in front of her, a small, conservatively printed sign read: *Madame Cosette Franck.*

Pierre was here to set up an account, though I didn't think it was in his name, or in the name of his alias. I stayed standing by the office door because I didn't wish to know any of the details. I heard Francine in my mind say: *The less you know, Dougay, the less trouble it can create for you.* At the door, I pretended to be Big Luigi, clenching and unclenching my fist, eyeing carefully people moving into and across the vestibule in front of me.

Pierre signed all the necessary paperwork and chose a PIN. Madame Franck arranged for a debit card to be mailed to an address—I know not where.

After completion, we returned to the hotel where I found the hotel's indoor pool and swam laps. I recalled that hotel in Montreux where I'd swum with Doctor Yvette Darvell, the gorgeous Swiss mountaineering guide who'd assisted me, in several delightful ways, while I was handling second unit work on Harold Kempenski's failed production of *Heidi.*

My memory of her was washed away when a woman dived in. It wasn't my Good Doctor, for this one was followed into the water by three children, who upon emerging, splashed and carried on laughing and screaming raucously. It was time to do an inventory of my bar fridge.

At six that evening, I met Pierre for a drink in the hotel's lobby bar and from there he walked me to a restaurant by the river where an excellent band played traditional Swiss folk music with an American country feel, interspersed with old rock 'n' roll classics.

People danced in front of the brightly lit bandstand, as waitresses in traditional garb juggled large plates of food between the musicians and the tightly packed tables. It took me back to an earlier time in Australia, to one of the RSL clubs where my friends and I had regularly visited.

Whatever became of those friends?

As Pierre had promised, the next morning we had breakfast, took a taxi to the airport and flew home to Nice. On the flight, he said, "It's time you booked that holiday to Türkiye. Madame Cartier is waiting to offer you a ten per cent discount at *Eastern Mediterranean Tours.*"

Like all businessmen, he sure knew how to keep up the sales pressure.

Chapter 5

Madame Cartier was everything her name personified—sophisticated, strikingly well-groomed with a touch of natural grey speckled throughout her dark hair. She wore a colourful cravat around the collar of her white blouse over a dark grey skirt. She could not have been more helpful, suggesting I fly to Türkiye via Rome, Athens and the Greek island of Samos.

"Have you been there?" She asked.

"No, never."

"They are so close, so nearby!"

"They aren't close when you grow up in Australia," I explained.

She understood and smiled. "From Samos, I propose you take the ferry over to Kusadasi in Türkiye. What would you like to do once you're there?"

"I only have one thought at the moment—to go to Gallipoli."

"Where?"

I explained the Australian connection to the Dardanelles. She tapped her computer screen, called up a map and zoomed in. "Oh, Gelibolu!" she exclaimed, upon finding it.

"I guess—I don't speak Türkish."

To get around in Türkiye, she suggested I hire a car. "Türkiye is a wide land, rather like distances covered in Australia," she said, before confessing she'd been to Brisbane for a world travel convention over a decade ago. She leant in. "I met a wonderful cane cutter there, in a bar in Brisbane."

"A cane cutter?" I asked. *Wonderful?* I thought.

"Yes. We had an enjoyable conversation. He was quite well-read."

A cane cutter? Well-read? I've never met a Queensland cane cutter; however, I was led to believe the only thing they read was the label on a beer bottle, and then only the large print on the front cover.

I proudly showed her my newly acquired French driver's licence and she said she'd get me an international one.

"I've just had a thought. This might be perfect for you." She stood and crossed to the young woman in the outer office. They chatted for a moment and then the young woman handed her a computer printout. She returned and sat again. "This has come through in the last few days."

"Sorry, Madame, I only read English."

"Ah, of course. There is a smallish bus tour which leaves Kusadasi for Gallipoli. It's recently been set up for those on the cruise boats, probably mostly Australians who want a chance to see Gallipoli. It's a sixteen-seat bus, not too large, not too small. It sounds ideal." She looked at the sheet again. "How fortunate! They have a scheduled departure two days after you arrive in Kusadasi. Before that, you could hire a car for a day. You really must visit the Celsus Library."

I told her she'd sold me on the idea, though the thought of being locked into a bus tour with packaged tourists was not exciting me all that much. *Perhaps they'll be a likeable bunch*, I hoped.

"Now, I recommend on the way over, you have at least one night in Athens. You must simply see the Acropolis. And on the way back, for the sake of balance, have a night in Rome. You must see the Coliseum. Remember in Türkiye to visit Ephesus."

"What's that?" I asked.

"An ancient Roman town. It's where you'll find the library."

I didn't tell her I wasn't a big fan of spending my daylight hours reading in a library.

She noticed my hesitant look. "The Celsus Library. I mentioned it."

I nodded as if I remembered, though to be honest she'd inundated me with so much detail I hoped she'd be handing me a printout in English, so I could study it at home.

"Ephesus is near Kusadasi where your ferry will land. The Temple of Artemis, one of the seven wonders of the Ancient World was there, right on the harbour."

"The Temple of Artemis," I said, trying to remember to visit it.

"It's gone now," she said.

Ah well, I won't be visiting that, I thought, giving her my credit card.

After she'd taken down the particulars, she said, "In a week, I'll have all your documentation ready. Any friend of Monsieur Legrande is a friend of mine."

At the door, Madame Cartier added, "I think you'll like the tour. According to this printout, it also takes you to Troy! Who knows, you may trip over some of Priam's treasure, or the body of the beautiful Helen."

"Madame, I'll be avoiding all desperate divorcées."

*

It was time to visit Gunther, the violent brother of Cecily. I wasn't planning on getting into fisticuffs with him, rather, I only intended to speak reasonably, to explain to him how his attitude towards Guy Franc will ultimately turn his sister against him. I wished to simply make the point that her life was hers and suppression of another's is the worst expression of care one could ever foolishly pursue. Anyway, that was my intention. I didn't get to speak with Gunther.

As I neared the address Guy had given me, I saw a hearse parked out front, and two undertakers lift a stretcher into the rear of the vehicle. From a safe distance, I removed my cap.

I observed the young woman, Cecily. She was ashen-faced, riveted to the spot, and staring at the stretcher. An older man in his late forties, heavy-set, dark hair, unshaven, stood by her. I watched the undertakers gently close the rear doors and respectfully climb into the vehicle.

Gunther tweaked his shoulders in a nervous, reflexive manner and returned inside, while Cecily stayed and stared as the hearse disappeared, deep in thought. I mused, *Dreaming of a life someplace else.*

I went home.

*

"M'sieur Pom," I said, as I pushed open the front door of the foyer, "can you do a favour for me please, all week?"

"Of course, what is it?"

"Check the Obituary Column, each day, please. Madame Valleaux." I waited for him to register the name because he seemed to know everyone in Nice; however, he said nothing. "I'd like to attend her funeral."

I started to head to the old iron elevator.

"I hear you're going to Türkiye," he said. "Before you ask how I know—let me say," he dropped his voice to a whisper, "Madame Legrande." He pointed to her closed apartment door. "If that's the case, I have something for you." He beckoned me with his skinny index finger. From under his desk, he took out an old paperback. I read the English cover: *Turkey on $5 a day*.

"Five dollars! How old is this book?"

"It was left behind, back in the seventies, when apartments in this building were leased as a pension. Some American tourist, I guess, had no further use for it."

"Why have you still got it?" I asked my curiosity aroused.

"I wanted to go there."

"Did you?"

"No. It's written in English. I couldn't find my way!" He laughed, enjoying his gag. "Take it. The prices are no longer correct though I bet they haven't moved any of those ancient sites."

"Thank you," I said, reaching for it.

He dropped his voice again. "Any chance of me getting back that photographic magazine I lent you of all those beautiful swimsuit models?"

"Yes. Sorry. I keep forgetting."

"If it's become the basis for your doctoral thesis, then surely the first draft has been submitted by now," he said, a touch of tease in his voice.

"I'm a slow writer," I said, more 'tease' in mine.

"A slow reader as well," he countered. "You must be thankful there are only pictures inside."

I headed to the elevator.

"Wait!" he exclaimed. He beckoned me a second time with his hooked finger. "Dougay, you're going to need to take a first-aid kit with you."

"First-aid?"

"Yes. Things go wrong. You can easily slip on a rock and cut open your leg—you never know. Wait there."

He went into his apartment, and just like on a traditional Swiss weather clock, right on cue his wife emerged. She came to me and kissed me on both cheeks. "Türkiye," she said. "I've always wanted to go; however, my husband, he'd never go anywhere they didn't speak French. In our younger days, I grew tired of flying to Quebec. Have a wonderful time, Dougay."

She went inside, as her husband came out carrying a small plastic container with a bright red cross on it. He unzipped it and pulled out its contents one by one, enjoying his little demonstration. "One bandage, one small bottle of iodine, one unopened roll of elastoplasts, one unopened package of band-aids, one gauze sock, one pair of tweezers and one pair of small scissors."

"Scissors? I can't take them on the plane, can I?"

"Yes, you can, if you put this kit into your check-in luggage. Make sure you don't put it in your carry-on bag." His demonstration and lesson were over.

"What happens if I trip and fall and cut my leg on the plane?"

"Ask the stewardess to kiss it better." He sniggered and leant into me, adding, "Don't mistake her for the steward!" He laughed.

"M'sieur Pom, sometimes you're a wealth of practical advice."

*

The following Thursday, the funeral for Madame Valleaux was held graveside at Cimitiere Caucade, southwest of the city, towards the airport. I'd been there some time back with Audric, a wonderful old gentleman, to visit his wife's grave. Their child had been 'kidnapped' and I'd managed to unearth the tragic circumstances around his child's disappearance and his wife's death.

It was my second funeral in as many weeks, so again I wore my dark suit. I may not be good at many things; however, I am good at paying respect. I timed my arrival, so the service around the grave was coming to a close. I didn't want Gunther to get suspicious of my presence, wondering what unknown distant cousin of his mother I may be.

The coffin was lowered. The priest sprinkled holy water and some mourners tossed in bits of dirt. Cecily stood off from her brother.

As the formal lines began to dissolve and hands were shaken and cheeks were kissed in comfort, I began to put into action the plan Guy and I had formulated. I approached Cecily and whispered as I passed by her, "Guy Franc kisses you in his dreams." To her credit, she made no recognition of what she'd heard. I circled the grave and walked slowly towards the exit in the distance.

Behind me, I heard heels crunching on the path. Cecily caught me up, and together we gently increased our pace, neither of us looking back. Outside, in the car park opposite the cemetery's entrance, I lifted her up onto the bench seat of Remy's truck. I climbed in after her.

"Let's go," I said.

Remy eased out the clutch and we hopped a little. Then the truck stalled.

"Come on," I whispered anxiously to the truck as if it was capable of understanding me.

Remy turned over the ignition again. Cecily craned her neck to try and see in the side mirror if Gunther had noticed her departure and was striding towards us.

"Remy, we don't need Cecily's brother seeing what we're up to!"

"Keep calm," Remy advised, becoming vexed. The truck kicked to life. All three of us breathed a collective sigh of relief and we headed downhill out of Avenue des Eucalyptus and left towards the city centre.

After three minutes, my mobile rang. It was Madame Cartier. "Monsieur Roberre, I have booked you on that sixteen-seater tour from Kusadasi to Gallipoli and back to Kusadasi which I spoke to you about."

"*Merci*, Madame."

"You can call by anytime and pick up everything. I look forward to seeing you again."

As I put the phone away, Remy asked, "Any chance of you focusing on the task at hand?"

"Sorry. I'm not distracted," I lied.

Remy stopped his old white truck outside *Gare de Nice*. A car horn honked as the truck shuddered to its final resting place, half on the pavement. Two taxi drivers further down stared at us with contempt.

"Okay, Cecily, let's go," I said, climbing down. She slid out after me.

Guy was waiting for us on the footpath. Cecily hurried to him. I let them hold each other for a minute before saying to Guy, "You got her suitcase?"

"Yes," he said. "She left it where she said she would. I picked it up after they'd departed for the cemetery. Her brother never suspected a thing."

"Good," I said, "Let's go."

"Here," Guy added. "Here's the front door key. Make sure her brother gets it back."

I won't be going anywhere near the brother, I thought, as I put the key into my pocket.

I didn't guide them into the station as they expected. "Where are we going?" Guy asked, stopping, concerned.

"Montpellier. Isn't that where you want to live?"

"Yes. How are we getting there if we don't go by train?"

I pointed ahead. On the footpath stood Jules St Croix, leaning rakishly against his illegally parked car, headphones on, listening to whatever second-rate music private detectives listen to.

Turning to Guy and Cecily, I said, "Go and have a wonderful life together." I pushed them towards Jules and lifted their two suitcases into the trunk of his car. One was heavier than the other. *Probably all Cecily's make-up,* I joked to myself.

As Remy joined me on the footpath, Guy turned and said, "You are the kindest waiter I've ever met! You're in fact too kind!" He climbed in the back seat beside his love, and Jules drove off.

"You are too kind for your own good," said Remy. "Your mother must have grown tired of reading you fairy tales at night."

"Yes, she did. She stopped reading them to me on my twenty-fifth birthday."

Most of the time, it's difficult for me to get a laugh out of Remy. This time was no exception.

Walking back to his truck, a horn honked belligerently at us. I was feeling exceedingly pleased with myself, having aided the blossoming of young love. So pleased in fact, I lifted the middle finger of my left hand and thrust it into the air at the honking car. In Australia, that gesture is very rude. I hoped it meant the same in France.

I clicked my fingers, suddenly realising. "Remy, drive me to Francine's office, please. I've an appointment!"

Chapter 6

I was a few minutes early. I waved *merci* to Remy as he drove off and waited on the footpath below Francine's office, gathering myself. A shiver of remembrance ran through me. I was standing in the exact spot where once two corrupt cops from Aix-en-Provence had beaten me to the ground and ran off. It is a rather pleasant feeling knowing, that after fifteen months, I have accrued definitive memories of a life lived in Nice, though I wish there weren't any violent ones to recall.

As I opened the door to Francine's outer office, I looked deliberately at the new shiny door lock. *Let's hope it works as well as it looks!*

The teenage receptionist looked up surprised. "Thank you for helping the other day," she said. "However, there are no jobs today." She eyed my suit and tie with curiosity.

"I have an appointment." One day I will have to explain to that girl just who I really am, though before that, I'd have to find out her name.

Two pairs of male legs stretched out from the chairs behind me. They belonged to Skipper and Matty from the *Blue Dahlia*. We shook hands, surprised at each other's presence.

"Any ideas?" I asked. "Why we're here?"

They shook their heads as one. I sat with them and we waited, me wondering why Francine needed to tell Skipper and Matty the date of her forthcoming marriage to the mayor before announcing it on social media. Through Francine's door, I could hear muffled voices—hers and a male—though I was unable to ascertain what was being said.

In the outer office, we all sat like that for about twenty minutes, waiting, quietly chatting about 'this and that' and 'that and this'. Francine eventually opened her door and beamed her most radiant welcome. All was immediately forgiven concerning the delay. We three men stood, and I let Skipper and Matty walk by me into Francine's office. I followed and closed the door behind us.

"Gentlemen," began Francine, "this man is Clarence Palmer, a partner in the New York legal firm, *Emerson, Loch and Palmer*." Now I knew why I was there. Francine did not speak English—I was to translate.

Oh, be careful, Dougay, I suddenly warned myself. *Is this lawyer here because of that brawl you and Remy had with that other American lawyer and his attached thug, that time they insisted Louise testify against Kempenski?*

Clarence Palmer said, "Pleased to meet you, gentlemen." I wasn't here to translate as he'd spoken in fluid French.

Francine went on. "You three gentlemen have been mentioned in the last will and testament of Mary-Anne Walton." I looked at Skipper and Matty, and they looked back at me. None of us had expected this. I breathed easier knowing the American lawyer's presence had nothing to do with Kempenski, or an announcement of Francine's forthcoming marriage.

Clarence Palmer cleared his throat. "Ten days ago Mary-Anne Walton's will was read in New Jersey. Her estate has been left to her brother and sister, there being no parents living and there being no children. Her entire estate, that is, except for the following."

He consulted his notes and read: *To Guillaume Delanche, the skipper of the Blue Dahlia and Matthew Dodds, the first mate of the Blue Dahlia, for their tireless work and particularly their belief in me, I leave them fifty per cent each of my yacht, the Blue Dahlia.*

Skipper and Matty were gobsmacked. I knew how they felt for a shiver ran up my spine as well. A tear came to Skipper's eye; Matty held his throat as if he was having trouble breathing.

Skipper whispered in awe, "*Mon Dieu!*" He reached for Matty's hand. They clinched—the two men visibly overcome.

"Our lifelong dream has come true," said Matty, breathlessly.

Turning to us all, Skipper joyously announced, "We now own our own boat!"

"Congratulations," beamed Francine.

I reached across to Skipper and Matty and we shook hands. They were quite overcome—snatched breaths, bursts of joyous laughter, and short statements of disbelief. Then in unison, they looked skyward and said, "*Merci*, Mary-Anne, *merci*!"

Clarence Palmer cleared his throat again. "To Douglas Roberts," Mary-Anne knew my English name! "I leave you the apartment…"

An apartment! Wow!

There was a real surprise in the room, none more so than from me because that was all I heard. The others had clapped in a spontaneous outburst as if I'd suddenly been named, contrary to Remy's belief, *Best Actor* at Cannes.

Skipper shook my hand, followed by Matty, Francine and Clarence Palmer. The room was flooded with thanks and best wishes for the future, all the while being mindful of and respectful to Mary-Anne.

Francine opened champagne, and we drank to all our good health. Clarence Palmer handed me a note with the apartment's address. I hadn't even registered if it was in New York or New Jersey, as I was so overwhelmed by the announcement. I looked at the address. The apartment wasn't in America. The apartment was here in Nice. I studied the street name and the number. Then it dawned on me. I'd been to this address before. It was the luxury apartment where I first met the screenwriter Philip J Phillips and the beautiful blonde Danielle Hubert. I trembled. Mary-Anne had owned *that*? And now *I* did?

"There will be a delay here, I'm afraid, Monsieur Roberts," said the American lawyer. "A legal hitch as we still have to do property searches here in Nice. We can't find among her personal items the deeds to the apartment."

I didn't say a word. Mary-Anne had given me papers, which I hadn't read because they were her private papers and therefore I felt I had no right to look through them. I'd placed them all into my safety deposit box.

I sure hope the deeds of that apartment are in amongst them, I thought as I stumbled out of Francine's office, with Skipper and Matty, not remembering much of the goodbyes. I took the two sailors over to *Vlatava-Elbe*, a Czech bar in the *Quartier du Port*, where the beer is cold and the slivovitz colder.

We drank. We cried. We told stories of Mary-Anne. We toasted her memory. We wished she was still here with us. I told them the story of how I met Louise, here at *Vlatave-Elbe*, the night she tried to run off with Mary-Anne's suitcase.

My mate Milovic and his brother-in-law Pasha dropped in. Milos, the bar's owner, had phoned and told them I was in attendance. Milovic had asked if I was once again with the international swimsuit model, Sue-Lin Cambridge. He'd been informed I wasn't, rather we were there having a private wake. The two came over anyway. They were extremely reverential—they sipped their first shot of slivovitz.

It was dark when we stood to leave. Skipper and Matty had by then missed the last train to Cannes, so Milovic phoned his wife and took the two sailors home with him. You can't do better than have good friends, can you?

*

In the bank, the assistant manager lifted from the wall my safety deposit box. She placed it on the bare-topped table in the room and bid me *bonjour*, leaving quietly, so quietly I didn't hear her close the door. Then again, I had other things on my mind.

I'd never counted the cash Mary-Anne had funnelled me in the weeks before her demise. At the time I thought she was being wildly generous, overpaying me because of some guilt she had for having tossed me over in favour of a pompous British film director. Now, with twenty-twenty hindsight, I knew she was stripping the loose assets she had around her, as her impending doom began resounding.

The bundles of cash were not in denominations of the twenties as I had assumed, rather they were all hundreds! The three packs each contained two hundred notes. Sixty thousand euro! I sat back and exhaled a long thin ribbon of air. Snatching a breath, I recounted it to make sure.

I moved the cash to one side and took out the papers. The first pages were held by a simple paper clip and contained the names and contact details of those people who'd regularly worked for *Kempenski Productions*. There were several names which meant nothing to me; however, I did recognise the names of Leon Williams (cameraman) and Lily Dodds (sound recordist). Next to Dr Yvette Darvell's name was written an address and a private telephone number. I didn't make a note of it. I wished the Good Doctor well. That affair was over and over meant over.

Closing those pages, I moved them to one side. *Today, Dougay, you have more important things to search for than carnal memories of yesterday.*

I lifted the next unattached sheet. It was the final page of the screenplay *Au Revoir, Mate!* Across the top Mary-Anne had scrawled in English: *Darling Dougay, for inventing such a memorable final line and title. Forgive me, M-A.*

Below the final line, towards the bottom of the page, it read: *Fade to Black. How ironic,* I thought.

There followed four signatures—*Harold Kempenski (Producer), Philip J Phillips (Writer), Sir David Tillman (Director)* and *Calvin deMarko (Actor)*. I guess Mary-Anne thought the four autographs on the final page, one day, would be worth a lot of money. One day maybe, though that day was certainly not today. I put the sheet safely back into my safety deposit box.

The deed to the apartment was there. "Thank you, Mary-Anne," I said aloud, kissing the document. I locked up everything. Outside the bank, I found my multi-day travel pass in the back of my wallet and took the tram over to Francine's office.

"I found it on the street," I said, passing over the deed to Francine.

She passed her legal eye over it and smiled enigmatically. "Thank goodness, Dougay, you and I have attorney-client privilege."

*

With my back to the sea, I stood looking up to the balcony of my newly inherited luxurious apartment. Well, soon-to-be apartment, just as soon as the slow-moving legal wheels ground to their halt. Francine informed me that it was managed by an agent in the Old Town and in hushed tones said that its tourist rental income was embarrassingly large.

I recalled being up there that first time, the door opening and the beautiful blonde Danielle Hubert walking by; telling me she thought the writer inside was Philip J Phillips, though she wasn't sure. That night I'd been impressed with the kitchen as I made an omelette for the three of us. Danielle wasn't that impressed with my cooking, and sadly, I was never to make another meal for her, to show her my other culinary skills, because soon after that night she'd been murdered.

Could I see myself up there, sitting on that balcony, day in, day out? Did I really want to move here and leave behind the friends and sense of family I had back at Avenue Auber?

No, when it's finally mine, I'll lease it.

*

Matty called and invited me over to Cannes Marina to have lunch on board the *Blue Dahlia*. I gladly accepted.

Walking up the rise at the top of Avenue Auber, I stepped automatically onto the pedestrian crossing in front of the railway station. A car blasted its horn, scaring me back to reality. I'd been daydreaming about my new apartment!

Aboard the *Blue Dahlia*, after a meal of quiche and salad, washed down with chilled champagne, Skipper and Matty became serious.

"We have a proposal for you," said Skipper.

Matty filled our glasses, as Skipper went on.

"Before she disappeared, Mary-Anne paid for two years' worth of mooring fees. So the *Blue Dahlia* is safely here until then; however, Matty and I are simple sailors."

I didn't think Matty was a simple sailor. He'd once thumped me in the kidneys and tossed me on board here, locking me in a cabin—for my own 'safety'.

"We don't have a large amount of savings, so our proposition is this. We believe we can make a go of running the *Blue Dahlia* as a private luxury cruise boat in summer, all catering provided as the kitchen is fully equipped. 'Privacy' is to be the keyword of the enterprise. We would take guests to any of the inlets on the French and Italian Riviera they'd wish to experience. We'd always own the boat, Matty and I, so we'd only be looking at setting up a business to operate the tours. And we were wondering, because we know you, and we don't want strangers coming in and taking over, if you'd like to invest."

I sat back and fiddled with my half-empty glass of champagne, considering what had just been proposed. Matty topped up my glass.

"Getting me drunk won't help!" I sipped and considered further. "That sounds wonderful, guys. What makes you think I can afford to buy in?"

"Perhaps you could take out a loan against Mary-Anne's apartment," suggested Matty.

I thought about their exciting proposal some more. They exchanged expectant glances while I concentrated on the sixty thousand Mary-Anne had given me before *Kempenski Productions* went belly up, and of course the remaining money I had from the sale of the diamonds and the sale of Gabi Surmount's pornographic artwork.

"Better than that," I said, breaking the hiatus. "Have I ever told you of my wealthy Italian aunt? I'm sure I can borrow the money from her."

Skipper and Matty relaxed markedly, smiling at each other, pleased the first hurdle had been successfully cleared.

"However," I said, "one small proviso." They stopped smiling, waiting for me to go on, wondering what new hurdle I was about to propose. "Yes, the boat will always be yours. That's a given, but in the tour operating company, I'd like fifty-one per cent." I had come a long way from the days when I was happy to buy into a café for five per cent! "I know you are lovers and I trust you implicitly; however, what if in time you had a falling out and insisted we have to sell the business before I managed to get back my aunt's investment or a worthwhile profit? I have to safeguard her interests, don't forget."

The two men exchanged glances. Matty nodded. Skipper spoke. "Both of us love this boat; both of us love living on the Riviera. The tour business will enable us to continue to live here, to sail our boat and give us an income. So we agree."

We shook hands.

"What should we call it?" Matty asked.

Indicating, with a sweep of his outstretched arm, Skipper said, "I have always loved the wide blue sea."

"Then that's it!" I exclaimed. "*Wide Blue Sea Cruises.*"

Skipper and Matty raised their glasses. I joined them. As we clinked, the three of us toasted, "To *Wide Blue Sea Cruises*!"

"I'll have Francine Delange draw up the agreement and create the company while I'm in Türkiye."

*

That evening, back home in Avenue Auber, I phoned Francine.

"It was really *your* idea?" She asked.

"Yes, Francine," I lied. "It really was."

"I'll organise everything while you're away." I think she sounded impressed.

She then suggested that she would ask the managing agent to let me inside the apartment for a sneak preview.

*

True to her offer, the following day, I met the agent, after office hours, in the street below the apartment. Surprisingly, he was standing there with Francine.

"I just wanted to have a look also, if you don't mind," she explained to me. "This, Dougay, is Monsieur Nardonne." We shook hands. He gave me his card.

"Welcome to my agency, Monsieur Roberre. I'm sure we're going to have a mutually beneficial relationship as the years go by," he said, with a voice which possessed the combination of Madame Cartier and M'sieur Pom. I trusted him immediately, which surprised me, for he was after all a real estate agent!

"When the titles are finalised," Monsieur Nardonne continued, "Madame Delange has arranged to inform me and then, immediately, we may begin leasing the apartment. I think you'll be very pleased with the rental return, even though we are coming towards the end of the season there is always demand here in Nice."

Funnily, Monsieur Nardonne did not come into the building with us. He bid us *au revoir*, handing Francine the keys. I followed her inside, into the elevator and up. She opened the apartment. Inside someone had catered a sumptuous meal, topped off with a loaded ice bucket.

This has overtones, I thought, *of a liaison I once had in a Cannes hotel with Madame Charlottenburg.* "Francine…"

"I'm superstitious," she said. "New possessions cry out to be christened."

"Is that you speaking or Madame Charlottenburg?"

Francine said nothing, merely giving me that enigmatic smile she employed to excite me. She undid her jet-black hair and shook it out in slow motion. *I wish she wouldn't do that!*

Chapter 7

It was Sunday evening, the night before I was due to fly to Türkiye. Pierre and Raphael Legrande had invited me, with the *proviso* I escort their mother, to a farewell dinner at *Le Grande Nice*, the first-class restaurant they owned.

Outside the restaurant, I took Madame Legrande's extended hand as she elegantly climbed from the taxi we had shared. "Madame," I began, "do you think Pierre will pay for the cab?"

Madame Legrande scoffed a delicate laugh and glided away to the restaurant's door. I paid the driver and joined her at the restaurant's entrance, taking her gently by the arm.

"Good evening, Maurice," I said.

Maurice Pontbriand, the Maitre d', has always ignored my greeting. "Good evening, Madame Legrande," he said, pointedly. "I hope you're well."

"Yes, thank you, Maurice," said Madame Legrande, the expectation of an enjoyable evening in her voice.

"I'm well also, Maurice," I said, though he didn't hear, as he had stepped off to lead Madame to the restaurant's central table.

There we found Madame's sons seated at opposing ends. With Raphael was the beautiful doctor, Constance Armand, who'd once x-rayed me after I was bashed and left to rot by the roadside with a cachet of cocaine up my ass, over near Aix-en-Provence. With Pierre was the gorgeous redhead who worked for him, and whose name I was destined never to know.

Also standing by Pierre was Big Luigi, who eyed me with disdain, saying, "I thought it was going to be an enjoyable evening."

Everyone stood as Madame Legrande sat. They ignored me, sitting before I'd set my chair under my legs. Pierre toasted his mother's presence. Everyone said how beautiful she looked.

"What about me?" I asked the others. "Who's going to Türkiye tomorrow?" There was no reply. "It's not a rhetorical question!"

Then, on cue from Pierre, they all burst out laughing.

Raphael stood and proposed a toast. "There is here in Nice," he began, "a man, who is the most suspicious looking, the most easily fooled, the most objectionable speaker of French, the most…" he let that hang. "And tomorrow we are finally rid of him. Ladies and Gentlemen—Dougay Roberre!"

They all stood! They all raised their glasses—to me! Pierre exclaimed, "*Bon voyage!*"

"*Bon voyage!*" everyone echoed.

Just how happy are they to be rid of me? I wondered. I confess, putting my cynicism aside, I was momentarily overcome. Madame Legrande said that I should say a few words. I stood and cleared my throat.

"I had no idea how you all truly felt about me; therefore, I cannot leave you. I won't be going to Türkiye!"

They all howled with mock disappointment, derision and scorn. I laughed out loud at their reaction. As usual, the wine that Pierre chose for his end of the table and Raphael chose for his was superb. Thankfully, I sat precisely between the two brothers, expecting to get inebriated by a combination of both varieties.

"Raphael," asked Dr Armand, "did you eventually find out the real circumstances regarding my burn victim?"

My ears pricked up. I leant a little forward so I could catch the entire conversation.

"Danny Bastille is well-known to us," explained Raphael. "He claimed his barbeque malfunctioned. His wife backs up his story. I inspected his barbeque, but there are no burn marks on the outer rim of the lid."

"Is Bastille his real name?" I asked.

Raphael slowly looked beyond Dr Armand to me. "Are you eavesdropping, Dougay?"

"How could I not? You have such a mellifluous vocal tone, Raphael, that all ears are drawn to whatever you say."

Dr Armand chuckled and patted my arm.

"I'm going to Türkiye tomorrow," I reminded Raphael. "How could I possibly interfere with or assist in a highly organised police investigation?"

"Oh, you'll find a way," retorted Raphael. "Somehow, Dougay Roberre will end up finding a way!"

Dr Armand laughed. She then became serious. "This man would have been leaning very close to the barbeque because his eyebrows were entirely singed off. Also, the fingertips on his right hand were burnt black and he had severe burns on his chest. He suppressed screams several times when I applied cream and wrapped his hands in bandages. He was a very fortunate man to have been discharged with those burns to his body. Still, we couldn't keep him there. With no burns on his legs and feet, he insisted on walking out."

"So," began Raphael, "to answer your previous, uncalled-for question, Dougay, 'Bastille' *is* his real name. A word of warning—stay away from him. He is unique in the criminal world. Even though he's made enough from his ill-gotten trades, he does not employ others to do his dirty work. It's a perversion he has—a hands-on love affair with violence."

The conversation was interrupted by Big Luigi tapping me on the shoulder and flicking his head, indicating that I should go over to Pierre Legrande standing by the door.

Dr Armand's mobile rang. "Dear God!" she exclaimed. "Really?" She questioned, not quite believing what she was hearing. "I have to go," she said, kissing Raphael. "There's an emergency at the hospital. That burn victim has been bashed."

"Danny Bastille?" Raphael asked.

"Yes."

I left them to say goodbye to each other and followed Luigi over. As I approached Pierre, the big Italian pushed open the door, and the three of us adjourned to the footpath outside. As if on cue, Luigi walked away a little, turned back and kept watch over us.

From behind, Dr Armand emerged. Pierre and I offered, "Good evening, Dr Armand." Luigi smiled at her, his face brightening.

Mon Dieu! A smile from Luigi? Where has that been hidden?

Dr Armand returned our farewell and headed down the street to where taxis waited.

"Don't make it obvious," Pierre began, "but see that man, slowly lighting his cigarette further up the street on your right? Do you think he's CIA?"

"CIA?" I whispered, suddenly sobering. "That's heavy stuff. Who's he watching?"

Pierre didn't say. "It's only heavy stuff in the movies. Those shootings and explosions, the things we've been brought up on, are merely the tip of the iceberg. Think about it, Dougay. Most of the work is gathering information, observing contacts and assembling links. It's a dull life standing around on street corners."

"Street corners? Don't they sit behind banks of computers accessing every corner of Planet Earth?"

"They still have to find out who and what to spy on. They still have to have someone on the ground to do the initial basic information gathering. It's hardly the stuff of Hollywood. Now, take Mary-Anne Walton, for instance."

"Mary-Anne?"

"If she were alive, someone in America would be searching for her. She is still wanted there."

"Surely you don't believe those charges, do you, Pierre?"

"No, I don't. Of course, I don't; however, those legal teams back in the States do. They'd be looking to find her—if she were alive," he added, pointedly. "They'd also be interested in keeping an eye on her close contacts. She spent a lot of time on the Riviera, so if I were a CIA agent, I'd start finding connections here. Particularly amongst people she knew."

Without moving my head, I slid my eyes to the right to get a better look at the man.

"And so my question is," continued Pierre, "do you think he's interested in me or you?"

"Me?"

"Dougay, remember to be vigilant, always. Not everyone will tell you that you've left your hand luggage beneath a seat at an airport. You're establishing yourself as a businessman here in Nice. You possess things now that others may want. I'm not saying he *is* CIA; however, some business people in this world love to know what other business people in this world are getting up to." Pierre studied the man as he drew on the cigarette.

Maurice poked his head out of the restaurant's door. "Dessert is being served, sir."

"Thank you, Maurice," I said.

"I think he was talking to me," informed Pierre.

Back inside, I was sitting by myself, my left hand in my pocket, fiddling with the small card Pierre had given me outside when Madame Legrande asked if I felt like taking her home.

"Of course, Madame, I have to be off tomorrow—an early start."

Maurice phoned for a cab and we said our farewells. The man who'd been hanging around in the shadows had gone.

Chapter 8

I was still wet from the shower when I answered my mobile. It was M'sieur Pom informing me that a hire car had called to take me to the airport.

"What hire car?" I asked him.

"The one outside our building!"

"Ten minutes!" I dried and dressed. I'd packed my bag yesterday afternoon, making sure the first-aid kit with the scissors was inside. I grabbed my carry-on bag and stopped at the doorway. I went through my mental check list for the final time, "Tickets, travel documents, passport, wallet and apartment key." I'd forgotten the old travel guide M'sieur Pom had given me.

As I was picking it up from my bedside table, Louise stood in my bedroom doorway. "Were you leaving without saying *au revoir*?"

"Oh, sorry! There's a hire car downstairs!"

"A hire car? There was a time you'd have been happy catching the tram to the airport."

"I didn't book it. I know nothing about it!"

She threw her arms around my neck. "Have a wonderful time and if you happen to meet a rich American divorcée, you have my permission to exploit her."

"Louise! You know I'd have to be in love with the woman before I'd exploit her."

"Go. I'll miss you, though not your terrible gags!"

Downstairs there was a gathering in the foyer. Milovic, dressed in his chauffeur's uniform was with his wife Ulna and her sister Ljuba. They cheered when they saw me, though Milovic being 'on duty' refrained. He merely touched his cap!

Stepping forward, Milovic, a formality to the fore, took my suitcase and began to drag it across the foyer to his limousine parked over on Rue Beethoven.

"Lift that!" shouted M'sieur Pom. "That floor's made from high-quality marble!"

"Sorry," said Milovic, and he carefully carried my bag out of the building, like the professional that he is, across Avenue Auber, placing it into the trunk of the limousine.

"Dougay," called M'sieur Pom, "leaving Nice today, you are probably better off—safer than remaining."

That's an odd thing to say, I thought. "What do you mean, M'sieur Pom?"

"A man has been found in an alley badly beaten."

"Beaten to death?"

"No, not to death. He was taken to the emergency department at the hospital where he did die—on the operating table of a heart attack."

I recalled last night Dr Armand had been called away to the hospital.

"Come on, Dougay!" shouted Milovic, returning to the foyer's front door. "You'll miss your plane!" He held the door open for me. Such service!

"Have you the first-aid kit?" M'sieur Pom asked.

"Yes and the old tourist guide."

"Good! *Bon voyage!*"

The apartment door behind him opened and M'sieur Pom was joined by his wife. "Have a wonderful time, Dougay."

"I will do, Madame Pom."

She kissed me on the cheek.

Madame Legrande appeared from her apartment, flinging her arms up in the air as she walked towards me. "*Bon voyage!*" She kissed me on both cheeks as Louise came running down the stairs.

"Bye-bye, papa!" she cried out, to the delight of everyone except me. "Come back with a rich widow so I can have a step-mummy!"

I didn't laugh. Everyone else did!

At the door, I turned back. "M'sieur Pom, what was the name of the dead man?"

He consulted his newspaper. "Danny Bastille!"

*

Milovic turned over the engine and we headed off for the airport, the two sisters in the back seat singing something in Czech and making flying gestures with their hands. After a while, I asked Milovic, "Where are we going?"

"To the airport," he replied, turning his head to me, smiling.

"No," I corrected, "this is the wrong way. Remy's warehouse is over this way."

As we passed by the Russian cathedral *Saint-Nicholas a Nice*, up ahead I saw them standing on the footpath outside his warehouse, Remy and Jules. Milovic drove slowly by. Jules held up a hand-painted sign which read: *Bon Voyage*. Remy raised a sign: *Don't come back!*

*

The flight from Nice left on time. The flight from Rome didn't.

I landed in Athens and the dry heat hit me as we were herded into an airport bus and taken to the arrival terminal. The driver drove as if he was angry at having failed the test for his formula one racing driver's licence.

Dragging my suitcase across the service road, I headed to the elevated train station. Madame Cartier had given me directions to my Athenian hotel, written in Greek. At the ticket counter, I stood and took the note from my pocket. I went to hand them to the woman, when she snapped, "*Neh?*"

"No?" I questioned, withdrawing the piece of paper.

She flicked her fingers at me. "*Neh. Neh!*"

"No? You don't want to read my directions?"

"*Neh! Neh! Neh!*" I put the directions into my pocket and turned away, not comprehending what was going on. I looked about, wondering where I was to buy the metro ticket. There was no other counter open.

She shouted at me in English, "Give directions to me!" I quickly turned and obeyed her. She ran her eye over the directions. Taking my money, she gave me change and handed me the ticket. "Change *Syntagma*. Take Line Two to *Acropoli*. Next!"

Aboard the train, I noticed a man sitting by himself. For an instant, I wondered if he was the man outside *Le Grande Nice*. Did that supposed CIA agent have a moustache? I couldn't recall. Perhaps Pierre Legrande was correct when he said that I need to become more aware of my surroundings and the people occupying them.

At *Syntagma,* I followed the ticket seller's advice, coming up from the *Acropoli metro stop* via a short escalator into the evening's summer light. I confidently set off.

I had no idea where I was, so I stopped and asked a passer-by, showing her the name of my hotel. She pointed behind me. Of course, I'd begun walking in the wrong direction!

Chapter 9

Waking early, I had a quick shower. Being on the afternoon flight to Samos, I wanted to see as much of Athens as possible before getting back on the metro to the airport. Off to the side of the foyer's small reception desk, there was a collection of faded tourist brochures and street maps. I pocketed a map and headed out.

My hotel was on the edge of *Plaka*, the Old Town, and so I decided to walk to *Hadrian's Arch*; however, it was not going to be easy. Ahead there was a wide road full of fast-moving traffic. Turning down to my right, I crossed at the intersection. The arch was now further away; however, in front of me, a ruined temple with impressive columns, some fallen, most standing, stood as it had for centuries.

Pulling out my map from my back pocket, I fumbled and dropped it. I bent to pick it up. Rising a little, I glanced at the temple and beyond that to the Acropolis upon the hill. From this position, low down, the traffic had disappeared, and I felt a shiver as I realised that this was how it had once looked, back in the glory days of Ancient Greece and Rome. I sat on my haunches and let the image from this position wash over me. The map informed me that I was at the Temple of Olympian Zeus. It sure felt like I was looking up towards the gods.

"Do you need a hand up?" A male voice asked in English, with a New Zealand accent.

"Are you stuck down there?" A woman asked.

"No, no, I'm fine," I said, standing. "I'm just imagining what it must have been like."

"Yes," said the man, pointing towards the Acropolis in the distance. "Very impressive, very impressive."

The three of us stood and stared.

"Well, nice speaking with you," the man said, and taking the woman by the arm, walked her off.

I crossed over through the National Gardens and walked from the Parliament into Syntagma Square. *Breakfast*, I thought.

Most of the restaurants weren't yet open, and the few that were, were out of my budgeted price range. On a corner, down the lower side of the square, I managed to find a food van.

I pointed to a pastry. "Sorry," I apologised in English, "I don't speak Greek." I held up two fingers.

"That's okay, mate," the vendor said. "Where in Australia are you from?"

"Sydney," I said smiling.

"Me? Melbourne."

"Ah, have you moved back?"

"No. I only come here for the Aussie winter to work for my lazy brother and to spend time with mum and dad. They emigrated years ago. I was born in Melbourne. Now they've grown old, they've moved back here to die. I stayed in Melbourne." He added with a broad Australian accent, "I married a dinky-di Aussie sheila."

He handed me two pastries, saying, "*Tiropida*."

"What's that?"

"Cheese pie. It's what you're about to eat."

I repeated, "*Tiropida*!"

"Bravo!"

It was my first Greek word. He handed me my change. "Ah, you've only charged me for one."

"Shh," he said. "Don't tell my useless, good-for-nothing brother. He can afford to be ripped off! Where are you heading?"

"Just walking around until I have to go back to the airport about two o'clock."

He pointed behind his van. "Down the street over there and up. Best view in Athens."

I thanked him, wished him well and headed in that direction.

"See ya, mate!" he called after me. I turned back and waved.

After a stroll down another traffic-laden artery, I crossed over and studied my street map. I took the path to the top of *Lycabettus*. Up there, Athens spread out before me. In the distance through the haze, I could see the sea, and of course, much closer, overlooking everything, the seemingly nearby Acropolis. I half closed my eyes and imagined ancient Persian ships sailing towards Athens hell-bent upon invasion.

"Oh, hello!" A voice cut my reverie. I turned and recognised the New Zealand couple from earlier. "We meet again," said the friendly woman.

"Yes!"

"What a sight!" her companion uttered. The woman passed me her phone. "Take our photo?"

"Sure."

"Three," she called to me, as I moved from them. "Take three, please!"

I did. She took back her phone. "What about a photograph of you two? I'll call it: *Two men surveying the Acropolis*."

"I don't think he wants to," said her husband.

"No, it's okay." I whispered to him, "Happy wife—happy life."

The man appreciated my philosophical gag. We stood facing her with Athens behind us. She took the snap.

I said, "If we're supposed to be overlooking the Acropolis, then we should have been standing around there a bit further."

"Oh, yes," she immediately replied, "silly of me. I'll take another."

We moved and she did, though this time she took three or four just to be on the safe-side.

"I'll send the best one to your sister," the woman said, playing with her phone. Why the sister would want a photograph of her brother and me I had no idea. It was as if the woman had read my mind. She added, "To prove he is capable of making friends!" She laughed. Her husband scoffed.

They bid me farewell and walked off, pointing at various things in the distance.

I sat a while, returning to my thoughts of the Persian ships and Spartans defending a bridge somewhere out there. My reverie was cut short—a group of tourists arrived! It was time to leave. Needing to check out of my small hotel by ten, I headed back the long way I'd come.

After paying my account, I left my suitcase in the store room off the foyer and headed out again. I wanted to hang out on the Acropolis.

*

The flight to Samos boarded on time. I think the same bus driver as yesterday drove from the terminal to the aircraft, for we hurtled around painted laneways, avoided baggage handlers driving tractors towing stacked trolleys of luggage, and thankfully, didn't slam into any parked planes.

Holding onto a pole with many other tightly packed tourists, I could feel my feet and ankles begin to ache. I hadn't realised how far I'd walked today. After the Acropolis, I'd headed down into *Plaka* and across to *Agora*, the ancient city's gathering place. Through *Monastiraki Flea Market*, I ended up at the busiest of roundabouts—*Omonia Square*.

The moment the flight left the ground, I nodded off.

The plane hitting the runway in Samos woke me. I hadn't even put back my seat for the flight, as I was still in the upright position. My knee ached and my legs were suffering cramps. I vigorously rubbed my lower limbs. *Oh, damn,* I thought, *I guess I missed out on the complimentary cardboard-packaged orange juice.*

I left the airport in Samos and crept forward towards the line of taxis, by no means at the front of the queue. Finally, arriving at the head of the queue, I watched the last taxi pull out. Behind me, an American man asked, "How the hell are we going to get into Samos Town *now*?"

His female companion said, "Patience, Miggy. I'm sure others will come along."

I turned to them. "I'm going into Samos Town. We can share the next cab if you like. I don't need an entire one for myself."

"No need, buddy." The man was emphatic. He didn't in any way require my generosity.

Please yourself, I thought.

"Of course, we can," said the dark-haired woman, correcting her husband. "Thank you, sir, that's mighty generous of you."

"American?" I asked, knowing full well they were.

"Yes," she said. "Little Rock, Arkansas! You can tell?"

I nodded, smiling, that I could. I got the impression that she might be up for a chat, though I knew he definitely wasn't. Perhaps he didn't like strange men talking to his extremely attractive and personable wife.

Twenty-five minutes later, a lone taxi sped into the parking bay. An ironic cheer rose behind me deep down the back of the queue. The three of us dragged our luggage over and climbed in.

"Samos Hotel, please," I said.

"Oh, that's where we're going," said the American woman.

The taxi drove off and after a while of climbing, drove across the ridge dividing the island and suddenly seemed to plummet down the other side, revealing the bay and port below us. The taxi driver drove along the foreshore as if we'd deliberately hired him to, and stopped by the ferry terminal. The Hotel Samos was opposite. Madame Cartier could not have organised it any better.

*

Changing into swimming trunks, I headed off to the rooftop pool. After some gentle laps, dodging children jumping in without care or parental supervision, I sat on a lounge and watched the late afternoon sunlight disappear. I read my five-dollar-a-day guide book.

The American woman arrived and stood overlooking the vista of the bay below. As she removed her summer dress, I looked away, the well-mannered gentleman in me instinctively coming to the fore. I returned my gaze as she delicately slid in, keeping her face out of the disturbed water. By the time she'd breast-stroked several laps and waved to me from the water, I'd forgotten all about the guide book. She climbed languidly up the ladder. I deduced that she was more Brazilian than American. As the water dripped from her, I knew why the husband didn't like strange men talking to her.

She turned my way. "A beautiful view over the bay," she commented.

"Ah, yes. Yes, it is."

"Enjoy your evening."

"The same to you."

She wrapped her towel around her black bikini and left.

I took a dive.

Back in my room, I showered and dressed. Downstairs I had a couple of beers in the restaurant at the front of the hotel and ordered *souvlaki*. Twenty minutes after eating, I took the elevator up to my room. I was too tired to go anywhere else.

*

In the morning, the ferry for Kusadasi left on time. On board, I was lifting my bag in front of me up the stairs towards the seating area over the stern, when my left foot didn't quite make the step and I tripped, falling forward onto my case, my left shin ripping against the metal stair. I cussed audibly.

Two hands grabbed onto me and helped me stand, uneasily on the steps. The hands belonged to the Brazilian-American woman.

"Thank you," I managed to say, as pain shot through my leg.

"Oh, you've cut yourself!" she exclaimed. Blood was trickling down my lower leg from the gash on my shin. I staggered up the remaining steps, hauling my case in front of me, onto a space on the bench. I turned and sat. Other passengers gawked. To her credit, the Brazilian-American woman followed and sat beside me. She intended to help me. I let her.

"I have a first-aid kit," I said, reaching for my suitcase. *How ironic!* I thought. I was glad M'sieur Pom was not here to witness this.

"No tissue in there?" She asked.

"No. I didn't pack any."

"Men!" she said, laughing. She found a tissue in her carry bag. "Here. I'll just wipe away the blood." She did so. "Now, put that elastoplast on it. Oh, you have iodine." I took out the small unopened bottle and she snipped the top with my pair of scissors.

"This won't hurt," she said. "And if it does, it's only pain." I thought she was joking, though she didn't smile. She ran some iodine over the wound and I grimaced. "Oh, don't be such a baby!"

"Are you a nurse?" She certainly had an 'I-know-what-I'm-doing' manner about her.

"Something like that," she said. "I've done a first-aid course back in the States."

With my scissors, she hastily cut a rectangle of elastoplast and carefully placed it over the wound.

"Thank you," I said. "Gratefully appreciated."

"You shouldn't die," she reassured me, again without a trace of humour. She left and went back downstairs. I hoped the husband hadn't seen and misconstrued.

As we entered Kusadasi Harbour, our ferry was dwarfed by several enormous cruise boats moored there. I wondered if passengers off any of them would be making up the tourist bus taking me to Gallipoli in two days' time. Then I had another thought. I fearfully studied every gangway. Thankfully, I did not see one rich American widow hurtling down them towards me!

Chapter 10

Leaving the ferry in Kusadasi, I didn't notice the Brazilian-American woman or her husband, though they had to be in the crowd lined up ahead waiting to get through immigration. Being the well-mannered person my parents had raised me to be, I waited until all the women passed by, before venturing down the stairs of the ferry, gripping the railing against falling a second time, through the lounge area below, and finally down the gangplank. I was the last person off the boat. Every man had sensed my upbringing and barged past, taking advantage of my good nature.

On the dock, a tall, thin, red-headed woman in blue jeans, white blouse and wide-brimmed straw hat, stood studying the large ships docked over from us. I indicated that she should go in front of me in the queue. She didn't smile, merely shook her head and continued to wait.

Once through immigration, I lifted my suitcase into the trunk of a taxi and showed the driver the name of the hotel Madame Cartier had booked for me. It was out of town a way, though right on the sea.

My room was up on the fifteenth floor. Flinging open the drapes, light flooded the room. An island out there floated on the sparkling sea, lit by the midday sun. A large schooner on the horizon eased across my view. I could've been studying a painting as everything out there was still and calm, including the boat which was leaving no discernible ripple behind as it slowly slid across the panorama.

Changing, I headed down for a swim in the sea. There were no waves, hardly any currents, so I didn't so much dive in as fall in. Stretching out on my back, I said aloud, "Welcome to Türkiye!"

I counted up fifteen floors from the bottom of the hotel. I saw my room up there, for I'd left my balcony door open. Three floors below, the Brazilian-American woman appeared, leaning against the railing of her balcony, her back to the sea, wearing the black bikini she'd worn in the pool at the Samos Hotel. I was amazed at how easily I'd recognised her. Must've been the colour of her eyes which had caught my attention!

I dived under the water and found a cold current.

*

I changed a small amount of euro at the hotel's front desk—enough to get me into Kusadasi proper until I found an ATM with a reasonable exchange rate. The manager said that there was a local bus—*dolmus*—which stopped nearby and would drop me off in the town centre. I took it. Once there, I found an ATM and loaded myself with Türkish lira.

Stopping by an interesting-looking restaurant, I peered inside. The room led into a courtyard with an open roof. A tree grew in the centre. Even if the food was only okay, the decor was certainly special. Cheekily, I wondered if Claude would like to plant a tree into the floor of *L'Opera Mozart.* I couldn't imagine him saying, *I'll think about it.*

There was a menu outside, and as I stood reading it, the Brazilian-American woman behind me said, "Oh hello!" with an enthusiasm only Americans can muster.

I turned. "Hi! You made it to Türkiye then?" I asked as if I hadn't seen her on her hotel balcony—the image of which will probably stay with me forever.

"Yes. How's the leg?" She asked, concerned.

I leant my leg forward as if I were some siren tempting a sailor. She looked at her handy work. "What have you done?" She asked, noticing the difference.

"Oh, after I went swimming, I was worried that the plaster might fall off, so I put another piece over the piece you put on. It should be okay as I read the label and it turns out to be completely water proof."

She laughed. "You didn't do a very good job. You've cut it every which way imaginable."

"I was trying to discover a new geometric shape," I said. She didn't find that funny.

"It looks lumpy."

"Yes," I said, "I failed First-Aid 101." There was no way I was going to make this woman laugh! "You're by yourself? Your husband's not joining you?"

"Husband? Oh, Miggy is not my husband. He's my brother."

"Oh," I said, her appeal immediately improving greatly. "I'm thinking of eating here," I said. "Would you and your brother like to join me?"

She thought about that. "Sure, why not? I'll have to wait for him. He's just down the street there getting money from the wall."

I glanced down to where I'd been. Miggy was walking towards us and he didn't seem too happy about something. Before he got to us, she began explaining, with a raised voice, "We're eating in here, Miggy. This gentleman has suggested it." She turned to me. "Sorry, I don't know your name."

"I'm Dougay."

"I'm Margarita and this, as I said, is my brother, Miguel."

I shook his hand before I shook hers. He seemed the type who expected it.

"Dougay?" She queried. "That sounds French, yet you speak English—like a what? South African?"

"Australian."

"Ah, Australian. Your kind loves travelling the globe. Many years ago— remember Miggy, that time I came here with some college girlfriends—I said I kept bumping into Australian backpackers every day?" She clapped her hands in eagerness. "So, Dougay, lead the way. I remember Türkish food as being delicious." She threaded her arm in through her brother's and followed me in.

There were two tables of locals seated under the tree. I headed for the empty table, abutting the trunk. "Oh, how lovely!" Margarita exclaimed. "Outdoor fresco indoors."

I gave Miguel the seat which fronted the tree trunk, while I sat opposite Margarita. He'd spent all his life looking at his sister, so I figured that tonight it was someone else's turn. The young waiter, no more than late school age, brought menus. "Americans?" He asked.

"They are," I said, pointing to my two dinner companions. "I'm Australian."

Without prompting, and as if it were the most natural thing to do, he wrapped his arms around my shoulders from behind and hugged me warmly, saying, "Anzac. Anzac."

I was overcome. I stood and hugged him from the front. We separated, and being unable to communicate outside of ordering a meal, I pointed to my heart and then to his, and nodded my head. He copied me, beaming. He went off to tell the older man, probably his father, behind the bar.

The two Americans didn't say a word as I sat back down. I felt a little embarrassed. "Oh—it's a long story," I managed to say.

The older man from behind the bar came over and held out his hand. I stood and shook it as he said, "*Hosgeldiniz. Hosgeldiniz.*" He ignored the Americans and returned to the bar.

Margarita wondered if we'd all like to go thirds on the meat platter with salad, yoghurt and pita bread. I immediately said I would. Miguel hesitated. I'm sure she gently kicked him underneath the table.

The food was served, and it was expansive and tasty. I fear I may have talked too much over dinner, telling them of my past year and a bit in Nice—though not the 'interesting' stuff—and my life back in Sydney. Still, Margarita didn't appear bored by my tales, though who knew and who cared what Miguel was thinking.

After dinner, I bid them farewell and walked to my bus stop, though I took a wrong turn. When I finally found my way there, Margarita and Miguel were waiting at the same stop.

"Are you staying out of town?" She asked.

"Yes," I said.

She looked up at me with her dark eyes and said, "Wouldn't it be funny if we were staying at the same hotel!"

*

I didn't swim before breakfast. I took the bus back into Kusadasi and asked directions, eventually finding the car hire company Madame Cartier had booked for me. I elected to take out full insurance, asked in which direction Ephesus lay, and tossed my carry bag onto the rear seat.

I drove up over the hill from Kusadasi; on my left, the Aegean fell away behind me. Berthed down there, two large cruise ships dominated the vista.

As I approached Ephesus, I passed *The Virgin Mary's House* up on a small hill to my left, though I didn't stop. I found the main car park at the lower entrance to the site. In my five-dollar–a-day book, I learnt there was an upper entrance as well. I decided I'd walk up to the top and then back down again. If Ephesus was as impressive as the book said it was, then two looks at it would probably be required.

Tossing my bag over my left shoulder and locking the car, I walked past all the stalls selling tourist paraphernalia, and pretended, for the benefit of all the touts, that I didn't speak English. I had no desire for either a cup of sweet apple tea or a carpet. Mind you, I could have done with a *flying* carpet to leap frog all the touts!

I did lash out and buy a straw hat! It was only a little after ten and already my head felt like it was melting in the heat. I was pleased. The hat immediately turned out to be an excellent investment. I paid the entrance fee and went in.

Slowing at a T junction, to my left, the theatre revealed itself in all its awe-inspiring grandeur. I stood staring and didn't hear the approaching voices behind me. Caught up in the slip stream of tourists, I was slowly swept along, hoping the guide would deliver his spiel in English.

Down on my right stood the Celsus Library. *I've found it, Madame Cartier!* I edged my way around the tour group and stood with my back to the guide. He was speaking English, so I looked in the opposite direction to which he was indicating, making out I didn't comprehend.

He moved on up the hill. I waited for the group to drift off behind him so I could feel less crowded. I turned my attention back to the magnificence of the two-storied, arched edifice of the Celsus Library.

Large stone steps led up to the entranceway, and off to the side I sat on one of the steps in the shade. I removed my hat and flicked sweat from my brow.

Another tour group wandered in front of me and milled around as if they were expecting me to address them. *If that's the case, they're going to be very disappointed!* I laughed to myself.

Their tour guide, dressed in a flowing cream top over faded blue jeans, pushed through. She held open, above her head, a red umbrella which doubled as sun protection and a beacon for her group in case anyone got lost. They were Americans. The guide said in her native twang, "In 48 BC, Julius Caesar accidentally burned down the library at Alexandria. To win favour with Cleopatra, Marc Antony rushed here. He ran up these very steps and into this very library and sacked it. He took back every scroll to Cleopatra in Egypt."

Marc Antony! Marc Antony ran up these very steps? I ran my hand slowly over the cool stone. The group walked up the steps and in. Not long after they filed back out.

On the way down, the guide stumbled, placing her hand on my shoulder to stop herself from falling. She apologised.

"Think nothing of it," I consoled.

Once her group had gone, I went into the library. Inside it was deceptively shallow. I guess it was only meant for storage and not to house large reading rooms, because back then, how many people could read Ancient Greek or Egyptian hieroglyphics?

I left the library, remembering to tread carefully down the deep steps and headed up hill. To my left was a group of German tourists huddled around a cluster of ruined foundations and dilapidated walls. One large man was standing in front of his group, making out to be a voluptuous woman beckoning his pals inside. Everyone was laughing, as only Germans in a group can. I noted on a plaque that these stones and rubble were the ruins of the town brothel.

At the upper entrance, with the usual carpet shops outside the ticket office, I turned and headed back down. After a bend in the ancient stone-paved road, I could see below the impressive edifice of the library, perfectly positioned. Beyond it, one would have seen the Temple of Artemis and from there the ocean as the ancient trading vessels entered and departed the port. I stood imagining it all. It wasn't too difficult.

Walking by the library, I entered the impressive ancient theatre, climbing to the top row of the seating. Below, over to my left sat the guide under her funny-looking red umbrella. She was eating her lunch, alone.

My leg itched. My shin was healing now, the scar underneath needing to be scratched. I didn't. I merely rubbed around it and tried to adjust the elastoplast, carefully peeling back the top piece I'd put on, before resetting it and pressing it back down.

On the stage below stood Margarita and Miguel looking up into the bleachers, shielding their eyes from the glare of the sun. They'd come to Ephesus for the day as well. I waved. It took them a moment to recognise my outline and when they did, Margarita returned my wave.

Stepping carefully over the stone steps, I walked down to the guide and asked if she could take my photo. I handed her my mobile and stepped away, down two rows, asking her to get as much of the background in as possible. Then I repositioned myself and said, "Those two people down there on the stage—can you get them in the photo as well, please?" The guide waved me along a little. She took the photograph and handed back my mobile. I climbed back down to the stage where Margarita and Miguel stood.

As I approached, I waved again, saying cheerily, "Are you two following me?"

Chapter 11

I asked Margarita and Miguel if they were as impressed with the theatre and library as I was. Miguel played it cool, which in this heat was no mean feat. I was coming to the conclusion that he was a bit of a party-pooper. Margarita gushed with enthusiasm, though she said that she'd seen it before, years earlier.

"Has it changed?" I asked dryly.

"No. How could it? It's an ancient site," she said, looking at me strangely.

Dougay, you're never going to make this woman laugh!

"You're right!" I exclaimed. "Nothing's changed according to my guidebook!" I showed her the cover.

"Five-dollars-a-day!" At last, I'd heard laughter from the woman. She should try it more often as it is very appealing on her. Miguel, noticing what she was laughing at, began to show an interest. Maybe he's fascinated with antiquities.

"Let me see!" he demanded, reaching for the guide. He fingered through it, briefly checking each of the maps contained within as if searching for hidden codes. "What does that mean?" He asked, indicating some names followed by numbers, written in black ink, inside the back cover.

"No idea," I said. "That's not my writing. Maybe 'Aunt Sally,' and that phone number, belong to the original owner."

Miguel handed the book back to me.

"I'm leaving now," I informed them. "The heat has finally won. I've got a car over there in the parking area beyond the entrance gate, and you're more than welcome to come back to Kusadasi with me."

"Thank you," said Margarita, without hesitation. "We came via a very expensive taxi."

"There's only one catch," I said. "I'm not heading there immediately. Down the end—there," I pointed away from the theatre, "is where the ocean used to be." I pulled out of my back pocket the free map I'd picked up in the hotel foyer before setting off this morning. "The sea is now about fifteen kilometres away. I want to go there and have a swim. Is that okay?"

"Yes," replied Margarita, then thinking, asked, "Miggy? Is that okay with you?"

"I haven't anything to swim in," he said.

"I don't think it's a populated beach," I explained, "so you could probably swim in your underpants."

"No!" Miggy was not the adventurous type.

"Look!" said Margarita, dragging out her black bikini bottom from her hand bag. I recognised it from last evening! "I'm prepared!" she enthusiastically exclaimed.

"Okay, let's go!"

We walked down past the shaded trees, through the entrance gate and past the carpet sellers, who suddenly became our long-lost friends. Foolishly, I let slip, when asked if I was 'American', that I was 'Australian'. A very persistent carpet salesman attached himself to me.

"I have a cousin in Perth!" he exclaimed loudly, holding onto my arm, hoping I'd buy the entire contents of his stall. "Perhaps you know him?"

I gently extricated myself, explaining that I probably didn't because Perth is four thousand kilometres from Sydney.

"I have a lot of cousins!" he shouted after me as if the Nullabor Plain was populated with a thousand Türkish carpet sellers.

*

The road became a sandy dirt track. I parked off to the side. Miguel and I stood outside the car, leaning against the doors, looking away towards the sea, while Margarita changed inside.

"It's getting hotter," I said by way of conversation.

"Not as hot as Mexico," he replied.

"You're Mexican?"

"Yes and no," he said. "I was born in the States though my grandparents are Mexican."

I didn't think Margarita looked terribly Mexican. I still believe her lineage may have descended from Rio de Janeiro. She climbed out of the car wearing her bikini and I now believed her lineage had descended directly from

Copacabana beach! My idea to come here for a swim with her just might be the greatest idea I'd ever had.

Miguel said, "You two go. I'll stay in the car. It's too hot for me."

"Okay," I agreed, without prompting. My great idea was getting greater by the minute.

"Can I have the car keys—for the air con?" He asked. I tossed them to him. His reflexes were impressive. He caught them without taking his eyes off me.

I followed Margarita over the hot sand. We were only halfway to the water when we could bear it no longer and we both started running, the sand's heat burning the soles of our feet. As if on rehearsed cue, we started 'oohing' and 'ahing' and finally laughed out loud at our childishness, as we ran into the water, our towels still in our hands, and the soles of our feet beginning to cool.

Taking her towel and cap, I walked back up the beach two steps beyond the wet sand. I dropped them onto the sand and removed my straw hat, shorts and shirt.

Running past her, I dived into the sea just like in those teen movies of yesteryear. I flipped onto my back and watched Margarita do the same, every piece of her doing the perfect amount of bouncing and jiggling that God had designed Eve to do. Maybe it was my proximity to the Garden of Eden which made me suddenly feel all religious towards her.

"Gorgeous!" she shouted.

"Yes!" I shouted in reply, not referring to the water.

*

The three of us took the elevator to the twelfth floor, where they got out. I continued up to the fifteenth. In my room, I dumped my bag and still holding my towel, went back down in the elevator and out of the hotel to the Aegean. I slid in. The afternoon heat was high, the water cool and I waved to Margarita up on her balcony on the twelfth floor.

She waved back and then raised her hand indicating that I should stay exactly where I was. For the moment, I had no intention of going anywhere else. She went inside her room and re-appeared holding aloft a beer bottle. I indicated 'yes, please!' I was definitely not going anywhere else!

Five minutes later, Margarita stepped into the water, wading out with two bottles of beer. We clinked and toasted each other's good health, standing chest-deep in the Aegean.

*

I didn't run into Margarita and Miguel that evening. I took the dolmus and returned to last night's restaurant. When you're on a good thing, stick to it. The father and son welcomed me as if I was part of the family. I ate Türkish pizza, washed down with dark Efes beer, leaving a sizeable tip because there was nothing phoney in their hospitality towards me.

Feeling sun burnt, which often happened in summer when the sun went down, I headed back to my hotel room and had a hot shower to help ease the sting. I closed the drapes, taking one last admiring glance over the Aegean and lay on my bed. What a day! Fabulous ruins; sitting on the footsteps of Marc Antony; saving a tourist guide from stumbling down steps; a hot overhead sun; a photo-op at the theatre of Ephesus; swimming in the Aegean with a beautiful woman; and pizza and beer to round it all off. *Ah, paradise on earth!*

Chapter 12

It was well before opening time when I returned the hire car. I removed my luggage from the trunk, slam-locked the driver's door, and slid the car keys into the slot in the agency's door as requested.

I had the bus's departure point, down by the dock, circled on the hotel's street map, and set off walking. As yet the morning was quite cool, though if the past two days were anything to go by, it wouldn't remain so for long.

As I dragged my suitcase unhurried towards the bus, I went over my last moments with Margarita on the beach below our hotel. We'd taken the elevator up, and on the twelfth floor shook hands farewell. I guess we'd both felt the same: that to continue was not a wise thing to do.

Two men, who I presumed were the guide and bus driver, watched me dragging my suitcase towards them. With my eyes fixed on the sixteen-seat van ahead, I missed the step-down and stumbled, dropping my suitcase. They watched as I bent to pick it up and right myself. With the plaster on my leg, I'm sure they thought I was not competent at anything which involved sustained walking or balance.

As the guide perused my ticket and checked off my name on his list, he asked in English, "Will you be able to walk, sir? This tour requires a lot of climbing up and down ancient stone steps."

"Yes, I'll be fine," I reassured him. I got the impression I hadn't.

"You can wait inside the bus, sir. Sit where you like. We have to wait for people on the cruise ships before we can get underway. Put your suitcase in there, underneath, sir."

I did so and climbed on board. I was the first passenger. I looked at the width of the seats and took myself down the back where the last row of seats straddled the entire width of the van. Sitting in the middle, I stretched my legs out down the aisle, tilting my straw hat back and trying to catch up on a few minutes of sleep which I'd lost since 4 am when I lay there wondering if I'd ever see Margarita again.

I heard footsteps at the front of the coach. That tall, thin woman from the Samos ferry climbed on, giving the interior of the bus a quick once-over. She gave no indication of having met me on the dock. Choosing the seat opposite the door, she slid across to the window and peered out as if looking for someone.

A large woman clamoured noisily on board. Once claiming a seat—the one immediately by the exit—she fussed about, lifting up and down her hand bag from the overhead rack above her, unable to make up her mind precisely where to position it. Then she got off the bus, almost falling down the steps, calling out, "Cyril! Get your skinny bum over here! Now!"

Cyril, his bald head appearing, stopped, catching sight of the tall thin woman in the seat opposite. He smiled at her. *Friendly kind of guy,* I thought.

He was forcibly pushed further on board by his wife. "On the left! On the left!" the big woman ordered loudly. "Yes, yes, yes. The third row. The third row. Don't you know anything?"

As poor Cyril righted himself, he saw me up back and shrugged, his look saying, *how could I possibly know? I wasn't here when you chose the seat.*

Two honeymooners in their mid-twenties climbed on. I knew they were honeymooners for they were joined at the hip. He quickly tossed their carry-on bags up onto the rack and they both fell into the second row from the front, diving down, cuddling and kissing.

I was immediately reminded of Guy and Cecily and wondered how they were getting on in Montpellier.

The coach seemed to dip a little towards the front as a big man with dyed blonde, short cropped hair and large dark glasses climbed on, missed his step and fell back onto his wife who'd somehow sensed that he would and had her hands out ready to break his fall. She laughed at his mishap. Clearly, they'd been married for many years.

"Can't help fallin' for my baby!" he sang loudly in a terrible Aussie–American accent over a poorly made-up tune. His wife followed him to the seat he'd chosen. She was dressed as if she was an assistant in a knife-throwing act in a second-rate rodeo, wearing a white frilled shirt with glittering chains around her neck and matching rings on many of her fingers. I took them for country music nuts.

Easing my hat down over my eyes, I wondered if the ancient sites were going to be any match for the sights on board this bus.

Another couple climbed on; however, by then I was beginning to nod off. All I heard was, "Terry! The back seat's taken!"

I was woken as the bus lunged forward. The guide was into his welcome aboard speech. "…Ahmet is our driver and I am Deniz. It is usual for everyone to rotate seating each morning and afternoon in a clockwise direction, that way everyone gets a view from up the front; however, as we have an incapacitated man in the back seat, I believe he should always sit in that seat as he can stretch out that injured leg of his."

Everyone turned around to look at me!

"What are *you* doing here?" A surprised Margarita exclaimed.

"What are *you* doing here?" A surprised me exclaimed back.

"That's *not* an incapacitated leg," commented Miguel, failing to deflate my wonderful surprise.

The coach headed up the hill leaving Kusadasi the same way I'd driven yesterday morning. As it stabilised and the road levelled out, I lifted myself up and wandered down two rows to Margarita and Miguel.

"Gallipoli?" I asked. "You're interested in Gallipoli?"

"No," said Margarita. "We took this tour to visit Troy."

"Years back I read a child's version of *The Iliad*," added Miguel, suddenly wishing to contribute to the conversation, "and became hooked. I wanted to come here ever since." I think in that short statement I learnt more about Miguel than I had since meeting him.

*

"There are over two and a half million people living in Izmir," the guide said into his microphone. "And I'm sure you're all grateful to first President Ataturk for introducing into Türkiye the western alphabet. In our wonderful country, you Westerners can read all the road signs."

"Yes!" called out the big country-music-loving Australian. "Though I still don't know where we're going!" His wife laughed. No one else did.

"Two and a half million?" Cyril's wife loudly questioned. "Half of them are driving on the road this morning!"

Margarita stood before me. "Dougay, do you have that five-dollar-a-day guide book?"

"Yes." I found it in my carry bag and handed it to her.

"May I sit with you?"

"Of course," I said, pushing myself up to allow her in beside me.

"There's a site I was reading about yesterday."

Before she could find it, as if he'd read her mind, Deniz spoke over the tannoy. "Pergamum! Our first stop will be Pergamum! It is best I say nothing about this, rather I let you experience it for yourself."

At the town of Bergama, the road suddenly narrowed through the village and we slowed considerably, though not long after, out the other side, we were accelerating and climbing. Ahead of us was a high commanding precipice. The bus wove its way around and up, slowing to a crawl behind a large tourist coach, changing gears. Another coach caught up to us from behind. Sandwiched between the two, our small bus slowly made its way to the top. All the while I looked out the side windows back over the way we'd come, taking in the view over the vast stretches of countryside. *From up here, Romans could easily have seen any marauding tribe approaching.*

"We have a long way to go today," said our guide. "Forty-five minutes here please, and remember to make use of the toilets. When you return, I have for you lunch. Some dips and breads and figs and dates and other delicacies. We will eat on the bus because we have to keep moving forward. Türkiye is a wide country."

Everyone climbed off, me being the last.

"How's the leg?" Margarita asked.

"It's okay."

"I see you finally got rid of that second cumbersome strip of elastoplast."

"Yes, I took your advice. It had served its purpose."

We all stretched our legs and shaded our eyes from the bright sun. The guide organised our tickets and we joined the line of other tourists shuffling their way into the site. At the opposite end of the entrance, there stood an impressive temple. I walked with Margarita towards it, Miguel tagging along behind.

I said to Margarita, "Tell Miguel, there's no need to follow me. I will not be seducing you in that temple over there."

Margarita smiled. "I think I am beginning to understand your sense of humour."

We walked around the temple, paying particular attention to stop and admire its detail from beneath, though only when standing in a column of shade.

Miguel began to fidget. "I'll walk back and buy water." He set off.

How thoughtful, I thought. *I'm getting thirsty.*

"Impressive, is it not?" The Englishman asked; the passenger who'd arrived on the bus while I was nodding off.

"Yes, very."

"I'm Terry and this is my wife, Donna."

"Pleased to meet you," I said. "And this is Margarita."

"Pleased to meet you both," Terry said. We shook hands and exchanged pleasantries.

Terry looked like one of those Englishmen from a previous era—trimmed pencil-thin moustache. I expected him to introduce himself as 'Major', though there was nothing fuddy-duddy about him. Likewise Donna, with short-cut dark hair and fashionable glasses, had a perceptive intellect about her.

I noticed Miguel returning and licked my dry lips looking forward to a cool drink. As he walked towards us I realised he'd only bought one bottle. He did not drink the remainder of it. Instead, he carefully poured its contents over his head and rubbed the cool liquid into his scalp. *So much for me and Margarita having the last two mouthfuls!*

"That's what I need," said Donna, "a cold drink. Come on, Terry, spend some of your hard-earned wealth." They headed towards the honeymoon couple, inspecting the stalls back near the entrance.

Off a way, four people emerged from a gap between large stones on the ground. I went over to investigate and saw stone steps leading down into darkness. I beckoned over Margarita. "Are you game?" I asked her.

"Game? What do you mean?"

"Feeling brave? Like to see what's down there?"

"Sure," she said in that distinctive way East Coast Americans pronounce it.

I led the way. My eyes adjusted and I turned right. Ahead an archway of light beckoned me forward. I stepped through it and out—seemingly suspended in the sky. I was standing in the back row of an ancient theatre built dramatically into the steep mountain side.

"Wow!" exclaimed Margarita from behind.

The view went on forever, the valley stretching far below. Down there, another coach was making its way up to us on the road we'd climbed. The theatre was not wide, the cliff face dictating its dimensions. I stepped forward to make my way down to the stage.

"You're going down there?" Miguel, who'd reluctantly followed his sister down into the sunken entrance, asked.

"Why come on an adventure and only experience half of it?" I questioned.

Way down below on the stage stood the country-music-loving pair. They'd not been daunted by the steep incline and the number of steps to get down to it. Unfazed, Margarita followed me down.

As we approached the stage area, the large Australian took an overly dramatic pose and with an outstretched arm called out, "To be or not to be! If that's the question, what's the answer?"

The wife laughed.

Seeing us approach, the large Aussie said, "Sorry, I get carried away. I'm Barry and this is my missus, Patsy Cline's number one fan, Dorothy or Dottie or Dot. She answers to all three. Me? You can call me anything you like—just don't call me late for dinner!" The big man laughed again and looking up to the top of the theatre in the direction he'd come, said in a poor American country accent, "I gotta go take this here stairway to heaven! Come on, Dorothy, Dottie or Dot. I hope you've been doing your morning bench presses because I may need carrying the last hundred rows." He turned back to us. "See ya!"

And with that, we watched them stride upwards, undaunted by the climb, obviously a lot fitter than they appeared to be.

Silence, thankfully, returned to the stage. Beyond the ascending couple, I made out Miguel way up there sitting in one of the rows near the entrance.

"Ever had a stage kiss?" I asked Margarita.

"I'm not an actress," she said.

"That's not what I asked."

I held out my hand to her. She took it, and we rolled into each other's arms and kissed. We kissed for a moment too long. I think she enjoyed it. I certainly did.

We broke apart and I said, "Take a bow."

She did. I made a point of bowing to Miguel and giving him a wave. From way up there, his animosity carried to me. Margarita made a point of our silliness by pushing me away—exaggeratedly, so her brother could see the gesture over the distance.

"It's time to go," she said. We assessed the climb before us and took a deep breath.

*

"Sit somewhere else! Cyril! I want to sleep and I can't with you jammed up against me like that!"

Cyril stood and looked about. He half-fell into the seat behind the tall thin woman, who turned and asked if he was okay. He said he was then she shot a glance at the overly large woman. *Was there a touch of the dagger in that glance? I asked myself.*

Margarita was now sitting with me on the rear seat, my map and old guide book balanced on her knees. From time to time, she'd consult the map, and with her eye liner pencil, mark off sections of the road we'd passed over.

"Do you know, it might be easier if you found what you're looking for on your mobile," I said.

"Yes, but not as much fun."

Fun? How could the sister enjoy this so much, when the brother was so bored by it all? How does one go about figuring out genetics?

"There are a lot of places we could see if we had the time," Margarita said. "I didn't realise there were so many ancient sights."

"Didn't you see them when you were here with your girlfriends?"

"My girlfriends?" She thought a moment. "Oh, we were also on a guided tour down through here. And back then, I didn't have your state-of-the-art guide book to inspire me. However, all I seem to remember is swimming at beach resorts and drinking. I was much younger."

Somewhere ahead, the road climbed into a wooded range and we stopped at a roadside stall, the braking of the bus on the gravel apron startling everyone on board. As our driver parked in the shade, our guide said over the tannoy, "This gentleman here has the freshest array of fruit and vegetables anywhere in Türkiye."

Sure, I thought, *and he's probably your brother-in-law.*

"Try a slice of watermelon. Highly recommended."

As I climbed out, the last one again, a dark car pulled in driven by two young men. They climbed out hurriedly and headed to the toilet behind. I knew how they felt. I followed them. One was in the cubicle while the other waited impatiently for his turn. I smiled at his discomfit as I fronted the trough. Upon completion, I washed my hands and joined everyone outside.

The stall owner had the sharpest knife I'd ever seen. In one perfectly timed motion, he cut off a piece of watermelon and handed the slices to us. We paid individually as we accepted each slice. The avocadoes took my eye. They were large, green going to black. I picked up the largest one and gently held it in my left hand as I dug into my pocket with my right for some Türkish lira to purchase it. The old fruit seller put down his knife on top of the other avocadoes next to his money pouch.

"Your knife, sir," I said. "It is very impressive."

"Yes, old, old, Byzantine, from the time of the sultans. Steel designed to cut off the hands of thieves with one blow."

Suddenly the two young men, now wearing balaclavas, ran from the toilet to the green-grocer. They hit him from behind knocking him onto me, grabbing his money pouch. I was unable to hold the old man with only one hand. He fell to the ground. The young men bolted for their car. I screamed, "Down! Everybody down!"

I hurled the avocado and it sailed over Margarita's head. *Plop!* It landed ineffectually in the gravel. The two thieves jumped in their car and sped away flinging gravel and dust everywhere.

I helped up the old fruit seller. He started shouting, walking after the disappearing car, arms outstretched, gesticulating wildly.

Deniz explained he was screaming about his lost money belt. I'd figured that out! Our guide said something to the green-grocer, placing his arms on him, trying to console him.

Deniz explained to us, "I see the car's number plate. I call the police."

Margarita carried to me the avocado I'd tossed. "It's bruised. I think you're going to have to buy it. You're my hero!" she laughed. I confess her new found laughter was no longer appealing!

Chapter 13

When we had washed the splattered remnants of water melon from our faces, we piled back on the bus and it took off. Terry came up the back and sat with me.

"You don't have the arm of your fellow cricketers!"

I didn't comment, not wishing to dwell on another failure of mine. "What's an Englishman like you, Terry, doing on a tour of Gallipoli?"

"Not Gallipoli, I've always wanted to see Troy, ever since I was a young chap; however, back then, I was only an apprentice and couldn't afford the trip. Then when I'd qualified—I'm a plumber—I got married and certainly couldn't afford to come. Then we had children and I thought I'd never get here. But lately, with the children grown and gone, Donna and me, we saved our pennies, and always wanting to take a cruise, we decided to hit two birds with one stone. Even though you missed the thief, it was quick thinking on your part."

Terry swayed back to his seat.

Sometime later, Big Barry took Terry's place. "I thought I'd wander up, get to know my fellow passengers. You know, friendly conversation, etcetera. It's been a long time since I've eaten water melon. Why do the great things you loved as a kid just disappear from your life when you get married?"

"Yeah, the last time for me—it was probably on some hot summer night back in Sydney with my parents in the small backyard of our suburban house."

"See? After you're married, it's gone."

"Oh, I'm not married."

"So that dark-haired woman is not yours? She's married to the other bloke?"

"The other bloke's her brother. I met them on the Samos ferry on the way over to Türkiye."

"Are you in a room by yourself tonight?" Big Barry dug me in the ribs and left.

A long way down the highway, our bus pulled into a rest area.

"We've still a distance to go," announced Daniz over the tannoy, "so please, this is a stop for the toilet and for snack food and drinks only. Dinner will be at tonight's hotel. I'd like to get you there before dark."

"Where's *there*?" Cyril's wife asked loudly.

"Cannakale," answered our guide.

"Never heard of it!" she rudely shouted.

Margarita swayed her way down the aisle to me and asked if she could have my five-dollar-a-day book once more. I gave it to her as we left the coach for the rest rooms. Stepping onto the ground, I rubbed the back of my legs and arched my back several times while I waited for all the others in front of me to complete their ablutions. By the time I'd zippered up, the coach was ready to leave.

"I knew you'd be last on board, so I bought you a cold fizzy drink."

"Oh, Margarita you're a life saver!"

*

"I've looked on my phone and *The Tusan Hotel* is about twenty kilometres from Canakkale on the Asian side of the Hellespont. In the morning, we take the car ferry across to the European side and then up the peninsular to Gallipoli." For a nurse, Margarita's mighty efficient when it comes to maps and schedules.

"When do you get to see Troy?" I asked.

"The following day."

The Tusan Hotel was where Margarita said it would be. There was enough light left in the day to enable me to get a swim in the sea, which I could make out through the trees, outside the restaurant off the reception area. I was the last to get my room key, so once inside my room, I changed quickly and headed back down the path through the pine trees. I waded out in the gentle cool water and slid in, floating on my back. The day's exceedingly hot and cramped journey was over.

Margarita and Miguel—yes, Miguel—found me there, and together all three of us stayed in the water for twenty minutes.

Big Barry stood on the shore beckoning us. "Dinner! Dinner in fifteen!" he shouted and hurried back up the hill. Miguel hurried out after him.

As Margarita and I were drying ourselves, she said, "I want to take it off!"

Has Heaven finally arrived here on Earth? "Pardon?" I questioned. "You want to take off your bikini? Here?"

"No! I want to take off that elastoplast! It's annoying me. It's half-off already."

"Okay, but don't hurt me."

She bent down and said, "I'll rip it on 'five'. Okay?"

"Okay," I said, bracing myself.

"One—Two—Three!" She ripped! I screamed! I hopped about in the sand, making out it hurt much more than it actually had. She laughed. "You big baby!"

I recalled M'sieur Pom's advice. "Kiss it better!" I suggested.

"Yuk!" she screamed.

*

Dinner in the hotel was a restrained affair. I guess everyone was far too hungry and far too tired to waste time on conversation, particularly the honeymooners who sat away from the rest of us, cocooned in young love. I'd asked the tall thin woman if she'd like to join me, Margarita and Miguel at our table. She said something about preferring to dine alone, as it aided her digestion.

After dinner, I excused myself, bidding Margarita and Miguel good night. On my room's small outdoor terrace, I took in a final view through the trees, before closing the French doors.

Is that the tall thin woman and Cyril down there walking hand in hand? It sure looked like them. I stood staring until the two figures passed behind a tree. "Huh!" I said to myself. "It most certainly is."

*

Suddenly the two young men wearing balaclavas ran from the toilet to the green-grocer. They hit him from behind, knocking him onto me, and grabbed his money pouch. I was unable to hold onto the old man with my one free hand. He fell to the ground. The young men bolted for their car. With the avocado still in my left hand, I picked up the green-grocer's Byzantine blade and made a rapid 360-degree incision in the fruit. I dropped the knife and gouged out the dark heavy seed with my rigid fingers. I screamed, "Down! Everybody down!"

I hurled the seed and it sailed over Margarita, hitting one of the young men in the back of the head and knocking him forward onto the gravel parking area.

He dropped the money belt. Staggering up he fell into the rear seat of the car as his mate accelerated away, throwing gravel over Margarita's legs.

I helped up the old fruit seller. He managed to say, "Okay. I am okay."

I called Deniz, "Did you get the licence number?"

"Yes. The police will find them."

"Thank you, my friend, thank you," said the old man, hugging me, his money belt secure around his waist. "Photo, take photo," he asked our guide.

With the old man's mobile phone, Deniz shot the two of us posing. In his hand, the green-grocer brandished his trusty knife. In each hand, I held a side of the famous avocado. When the photo had been taken, the old fruit seller rewarded me by giving every one of us an extra slice of watermelon. "You very quick-thinking American," he said to me.

"Australian, not American."

"Australian? Anzac?" He threw his arms around me not wanting to let me go.

Back at the coach, all the passengers congratulated me. "You're our hero!" Margarita blew me a kiss. The tall thin woman came up to the back seat, seductively swaying her hips and straddled me! She pulled out the green-grocer's Byzantine knife and raised it over my head.

I snapped awake!

I'm not a fan of dreams. Sometimes they disturb me.

*

After breakfast, the bus carried us to Canakkale, down the main street to the car ferry. We were towards the front of the traffic queue, so some of us waited on the footpath watching the boat come across the water. The honeymooners stood hand in hand off to one side of our small gathering.

Big Barry, as if reading my thoughts, sang quietly for my benefit, "Young love, first love, filled with true devotion." I nodded in appreciation and having got his desired response, he walked back to his wife.

The tall thin woman again stood alone. I decided to be friendly, drifting over and saying, "I'm Dougay," I held out my hand. "What's your name?"

"Yootha," she said curtly, not taking my out stretched hand.

"That's a rare name," I commented, withdrawing it.

"Yes." She walked off, up into the bus. Cyril, unbeknownst to his wife, watched her go. I sauntered over.

"So, Cyril, what do you do?"

"I'm an accountant—for my wife. Many years ago, she opened a beauty salon in our suburb. Then with the success of that, she opened up one in the neighbouring suburb and then with the success of that..." Cyril found a business card in his wallet. It read: *Desli's. The House of Beauty. Glamourising Western Sydney.*

I had to restrain myself from laughing. As I handed back his card, I could only say, "Impressive!" as Desli was one of the most unattractive women I had ever seen!

Deniz beckoned us all back on board; our bus carefully driving onto the ferry. Once it was safely parked, we all climbed out and found seats up on deck in the open air.

As the ferry pulled out, Margarita read from my old guide book. "Lord Byron swam across here," she informed us, "at the Hellespont's narrowest point."

Miguel studied the current. "He'd have had to have judged the turn in the tide perfectly," he told his sister, doubting what she'd read. By contrast, being a swimmer, I admired the poet's feat.

On the European side, our bus drove through Eceabat and north up the peninsula. The road narrowed into Gallipoli and our driver dropped the vehicle's pace accordingly.

"What do you expect to find in here?" Margarita asked.

"I don't know," I answered, truthfully. What I did know, was that for the past fifteen minutes, I had become subdued. Was it trepidation? Cautiousness? The weight of Australian history?

The trees gave way to a parking area and our bus pulled in. Getting out, we all milled by the entrance, hesitant, fearing, or respecting what we'd find. I assume Margarita and Miguel followed. I had no idea what the others were doing because I was now moving forward as if in a cocoon. In front was Anzac Cove and I walked there, carefully, each footstep not wishing to disturb the ground.

Ataturk's sign caught my eye; however, I refused to read it in detail for the moment. I walked onto the narrow pebbled sandy beach and listened to the rhythmically quiet plop of the water on the shoreline. I looked up to my right, inland, and was surprised to see the height of the cliffs. They were much smaller than I'd imagined.

The other Australians were also caught up in their emotions, stepping carefully along the narrow beach, trying not to kick the pebbles or in any way disturb the ground.

The honeymooners came to a stop nearby. The young woman took a paper flower from inside her jacket and stepped to the water, tossing it out in an upward motion. It held in the air a moment then gently fell to the sea. She stepped back and turned to me. "In memory of my great-great-grandfather." She then took her husband's arm and they walked off.

Deniz quietly gathered us together. "Lone Pine, come, we go. Do not worry. We will come back here before we leave the site. In the past, I have found that people prefer that."

Back on the bus, I didn't speak to Margarita and she didn't ask me any questions. I sat in a sort of contented silence, reflecting on what, I couldn't put my finger on. As the coach climbed carefully up the road, out the side windows I noticed overgrown trenches dug into the ground.

We stood in the area by the lone tree. I took my old guide book from Margarita and read what little it had to say about the site. I guess the memorial hadn't been constructed back when the book had been published. I gave it back to her and started to walk off.

"Can I come with you?" She asked.

I stopped and turned. "Yes, of course you can. Sorry, I guess I'm distracted."

We crossed the stone paving, walking to the far wall. We turned back to study another angle of the tree.

"He's the one!" I heard the young woman's voice say from behind the wall. Margarita looked quizzically at me. I shrugged, having no idea what the honeymooners could possibly be talking about.

Ahmet drove the loop back down to Anzac Cove and I studied in greater detail the overgrown trenches from 1917. They weaved about. I'd always thought that somehow they'd be straight and in parallel.

I walked again the narrow sand at Anzac Cove and read in detail Ataturk's words mounted there.

You, the mothers who sent their sons from faraway countries, wipe away your tears. Your sons are now lying in our bosom and are in peace. After having lost their lives on this land, they have become our sons as well.

It was then, in that silence, tears emerged. I didn't brush them away. I don't know if Margarita noticed. I didn't care. For the past eighteen months, I'd been telling myself that I was French. Perhaps I've been deluding myself. Perhaps I'm more Australian than I'd ever appreciated. I looked out over that calm sea and back up to the stunted hills behind me and imagined the slaughter.

*

I was lying in the cool water below *The Tusan Hotel*. As in Kusadasi, Margarita carried down two beers into the water. She could have been crossing the sand of Copacabana beach, for she sure turned my head. I sang to myself, *Tall and tanned and young and lovely...*

Dinner, once again in the hotel, was a much noisier affair than last night. It was as if Gallipoli had bonded us and its aftermath had loosened everyone's tongues.

Big Barry came around and whispered to each of us in turn. "I'm putting together a collective tip for Ahmet and Deniz. They've been really helpful and efficient. No, not now. I'll collect it over breakfast."

"Why halfway through the tour?" I asked.

"The honeymooners are leaving us in the morning. Deniz said that they have a flight to catch in Istanbul. Ahmet will take them into Cannakale's long-distance bus station after breakfast." He then sang, "Take me home, country roads..."

After dinner, Terry suggested we all gather at the bar of a fish restaurant down on the water. Everyone attended, except the young honeymooners and Desli who went off to her usual early bed.

"What do you do, Margarita?" Big Barry asked. "For a crust?"

"For a crust?" She asked, not understanding.

Before he could explain, I butted in. "She's a nurse. In fact, I can vouch for her professionalism. On the ferry over to Türkiye from Samos, I tripped and gashed my leg. Margarita bandaged me up."

"Nursing," mused Big Barry. "Yeah, I wish I had a trade, though I can't complain. I was born and bred on the land, and inherited a fifth-generation homestead."

"Sheep or cattle?" I asked.

"Not anymore. I sold it off to a Chinese mining company. You should have seen my eyes when they told me what they were offering." He sang, "Crazy, crazy for feeling so wealthy."

He didn't finish for his wife Dorothy, Dottie or Dot grabbed him by the arm. "Big Barry Baby, are you singing a Patsy song?"

Then without prompting, and in perfect sync, they sang, "You walk by and I fall to pieces."

*

And so a very enjoyable evening of conversation and enthusiastically sung snatches of country songs proceeded.

Miguel, making it more enjoyable, left halfway through Big Barry's full rendition of *Crazy*. On his way out, I caught his warning look at Margarita. *What could he possibly be giving her caution about?*

Later, when we'd all had enough and were leaving, I held Margarita off to one side and said quietly, fighting my drunkenness, "Margarita, if you flew away during the night, I'd have no way of ever contacting you."

She thought about that. In her purse, she found her black eye liner pencil. "Do you have paper?" She asked. I didn't. Then an idea hit me from left field. I recalled the time Eloise Pittard had written her contact number on a euro note. I searched my wallet and took out a red ten lira note. Margarita took it from me and scrawled on it a set of large lopsided numbers. I looked at them and smiled back at her. "Thank you," I said, returning the note to my wallet. In the morning, when I'd sobered, I'd no doubt make sense of the numerals she'd written there.

*

It was very dark and I was trying to wake up. There was someone in the room standing near my bed head. I lashed out and hit savagely some part of a body. The person stifled a grunt and clutched up the things on my bedside table. My sudden movement sent my head spinning.

I couldn't find my legs, as one was on top of the sheet and the other below it.

The intruder fled across the room and out through the French doors. By the time I got to them, there was no movement outside. I held myself against the door frame trying not to fall. I looked at my watch: *4.17 a.m.* I found the room's light and checked my bedside table. My wallet had been taken.

94

I stumbled about the room, wondering if, during the scuffle, it had been dropped. It had, outside on the small patio, though it hadn't been dropped, it had been discarded. I opened it. My cards were all in place though I'd been cleaned out of cash—the equivalent of about four hundred euros!

Chapter 14

It took me a long while to get back to sleep.

You idiot, Dougay! Why did you leave the French doors open? It was hot, that's why! Why didn't you hear the intruder? Because you were drunk, you idiot! Why do you never learn? Bloody idiot, idiot, idiot!

I walked into breakfast sheepishly looking for Margarita to tell her what had happened. Before I could get to her, Big Barry approached. "Money for the tip?"

"Huh?"

"Money for the tip for Ahmet and Deniz. Remember? I asked you last night?"

"Oh, yes." I instinctively reached for my wallet. Of course, it was empty. "In a minute, Barry, I've just got to check with Margarita something she wanted me to do this morning," I lied.

Crossing to her table, I ignored Miguel and whispered in Margarita's ear. "Can I see you over there, please?" I pointed to the back of the dining room.

"Of course," she said and followed me, curious as to why.

"At four this morning, an intruder came into my room and robbed me of all my cash, the equivalent of four hundred euros! I was wondering if I could borrow enough this morning for the tip—you know, the collective tip for the driver and the guide that Big Barry is organising."

"Of course," she said, sympathetically. "But who? You don't think one of us could have done it, do you?"

"I don't know. I managed to hit him. I landed a blow to the thigh region. Anyone walk in here this morning with a limp?"

She was unable to reply as Big Barry was suddenly next to her. "Money for the tip, please, Margarita?"

"Of course," she wandered back to her table.

Big Barry eyed her and sang, "I've got your records and she's got you." He then clicked his tongue, suggestively.

Margarita returned and handed him some cash, saying, "This is for Miguel and me *and* Dougay."

Big Barry raised his eyebrows at me, thanked her and made his way to the front of the breakfast room as Ahmet helped lift the bags of the honeymoon couple out the door and to the bus parked outside.

Big Barry called for attention, announcing, "Everyone! Congratulations on the effort! This here, in my hot little hand, is the tip!" He waved a wad of notes in the air, fanning them out so we all could see our contribution. "Hey!" he shouted good-naturedly to the departing honeymoon couple. "You haven't left your tip for Ahmet and Deniz!"

"Ah!" said the young man, caught in a moment of spot-lit embarrassment. He put down his shoulder bag and quickly dug into his wallet. He thrust a note into Big Barry's hand, picked up his shoulder bag and the two of them left for the bus.

"Best of luck in life!" shouted Desli. "If you're ever in Western Sydney, look me up. I'll give you a free manicure!" The honeymooners didn't turn back to indicate they had heard her offer of a lifetime.

Big Barry lifted the complete tip into the air and waved it again. "Congratulations! It's a most generous gesture on your, and my part."

People began to applaud. Margarita began to run. She took off out the front of the restaurant and through the hotel's reception. I headed to a window to see what she was up to. The bus was pulling away, when she banged on its door. It stopped, the door opened up and Margarita hopped on. It drove off!

"Where's Margarita gone?" Miguel asked, joining me at the window.

"I have no idea."

He stared out at the disappearing bus. With the look he gave it, I wondered if Margarita had finally had enough of her unfriendly brother and planned on taking a long-distance bus to Istanbul!

We both sat at Miguel's table and had breakfast. As usual, no conversation ensued.

On my third cup of coffee, about forty minutes later, I heard our bus pull up outside. Miguel by now had disappeared. Margarita came back into the hotel's dining room, a look of extreme satisfaction on her face. She sat and slapped down on the table in front of me about four hundred euros in Turkish lira.

"There was no need to go to a Hole-in-the-Wall," I said. "I could have done that later today."

"Didn't you see?" She asked.

"See what?"

"Big Barry. He held up those notes for Ahmet's and Deniz's tips. Then he was handed the tip from the honeymooners and waved it again."

"So?" I asked.

"Clearly visible was your note—the one I wrote my contact number on last night."

"Barry? Big Barry stole my money?"

"No. You are more hungover than I thought. Not Big Barry. The honeymooners! They were making their getaway this morning!"

I looked at her unbelievingly. "The honeymooners?"

"Yes. The woman is walking with a limp, courtesy of you. The man tried bluff and bravado, but Ahmet understanding what I was accusing them of, stopped the bus, refusing to take them to the bus station. There was a standoff, until the honeymooners realised they'd miss their connection to Istanbul."

"You're a wonder, Margarita."

"Drink your coffee, Dougay, or you'll make us late for Troy."

*

Our bus headed south about thirty kilometres to the town of Hisarlik. Ahmet turned off the highway. We pulled up at the ticket office, and further on stopped in the parking bay.

Big Barry stood in the aisle of the coach not letting anyone out. "I'm Agamemnon and fellow Greeks follow me as we ransack Troy and rescue the beautiful Helen!"

"Maybe I don't want to be rescued!" announced Desli.

It must have been a whole two minutes before the laughter on board the bus died sufficiently to allow people to find their feet and disembark.

Outside the coach, Terry wiped tears from his eyes and whispered to me, "Desli—the face that sunk a thousand ships."

"Is that the original horse?" Dorothy asked.

"No," said Deniz. "It's a tourist mock-up. The original wood rotted away centuries ago." I wondered how many times over the years he'd answered that question and managed to keep a straight face.

I confess I was still in a bit of a daze and the overhead sun wasn't helping. My hungover head was back there at Gallipoli, and what grey cells hadn't been damaged last night were trying to figure out why the young couple had chosen me as their target. *Do I look and behave like an easy mark? I guess I do.*

I followed everyone around the site, taking up my usual position at the rear. Donna and Terry, happy to be here at last, walked side by side pointing and commenting, reading their guide book to the site and taking many photos on their phones. Big Barry was whistling some country tune and Dot was providing an occasional interspersed lyric.

Cyril stumbled on a rock and fell. Desli turned as Yootha stepped forward and helped him to his feet.

"Watch what you're doing, Cyril!" admonished Desli, unconcerned with the image of Yootha's arms around her husband, helping him. "Those rocks are ancient. Don't damage them! They've history written all over them, and you can't read ancient Egyptian!"

Deniz led us to the ramp leading to where he said the main gate once stood.

"I'd say this led to the main gate," informed Miguel, consulting my old guide book over Margarita's shoulder.

"Weren't you just listening?" Margarita asked. "At times, Miguel, you seem to live in a parallel world."

Hasn't she figured that out by now? I pondered. *They've only been brother and sister for thirty-something years!*

After an hour and a half of wandering around, reading plaques and consulting tourist maps of the site, Deniz gathered us all together and said it was time to go. "We have a long trip ahead of us. We'll only be stopping for a quick lunch and toilet breaks."

Donna and Terry reluctantly climbed on board. I hoped their long-held dream had been satisfied.

Ahmet carefully drove our bus out between the large tourist coaches, dodging pedestrians and running children, eager to climb inside the 'Trojan Horse'. Margarita came and joined me in the back seat as Big Barry and Dorothy sang, "Hit the road, Jack."

*

Back in Kusadasi, down by the big cruise boats, we took a farewell group photo in front of our bus, waving farewell to Ahmet and Deniz. Forming a large circle with suitcases at our feet, we stood there for a while, individuals saying goodbyes and promising one day to catch up, even though we all lived several thousands of kilometres away from each other.

"Big Barry, you and Dot keep pumping out those songs."

"Too right, Dougay. Will do. I'll sing them extra loud so you'll hear them in France. See ya, mate!"

"See ya, Dougie!" said Dot, giving me a peck on the cheek.

They picked up their suitcases and headed off towards the dock where their gigantic cruise ship was moored. The last I heard of them was the sung line, "On the road again…"

I wished Donna and Terry the best of luck.

"Same to you, Dougay."

"Pleased you finally made it to Troy?"

"Yes, though we could've stayed there a week," said Donna.

I waved *au revoir* to Yootha. She didn't return my gesture.

Shaking Cyril by the hand, I said, "A pleasure meeting you. Take care, Cyril."

"You too, Dougay."

I went to bid Desli *au revoir* also; however, she was waddling off to her waiting cruise ship, desperate to get her head down on her bunk.

Cyril gave Yootha a yearning look. She took a tentative half step to him; however, he turned from her and headed off after his wife, his shoulders slumped, dragging both their suitcases.

"Share a taxi with us, Yootha?" I asked.

She shook her head and stood watching Cyril walk away.

Everyone deals with goodbyes in their own particular way, I assessed. However, I did wonder how I was going to feel when it was time to farewell Margarita.

*

As we were checking into the same hotel, I asked Margarita if she'd like to have dinner with me. I didn't mention Miguel. I couldn't care less where or what he ate. I'd had enough of his gloomy presence. She accepted. She didn't mention her brother either. We took the dolmus together from our hotel into Kusadasi.

"How about the tree restaurant?" I asked her.

"Sure," she smiled. "You just want to be hugged by that young man again."

"I'd rather be hugged by you," I admitted, cheekily.

She wove her arm through mine and we walked together like that, the evening light fading over the mountain behind us. Outside the restaurant, the young man clapped his hands in recognition as we approached. He called out to his father. After a round of hugging, we were shown to 'our table' next to the tree.

"You're quite a gregarious man, aren't you?" Margarita said as I moved her chair out from the table so she could sit.

I made no comment about that. "Margarita, you order," I said, "Whatever takes your fancy—my shout."

"You are going to scream?" She asked.

"No, no," I laughed. "It's an Australian expression. It means that I'll pay the bill."

"That's mighty generous of you, sir," she said in a put-on western accent. I was reminded of Mary-Anne when she'd speak to me in her embellished New Jersey twang.

As Margarita took her first sip, I said, "I'll never forget you bringing that beer down from your hotel room to me in the water." She said nothing. Maybe it wasn't such a big deal for her; however, I knew it had made a lasting impression on me. "I'll also never forget you running into the sea to relieve that burning sand underfoot." I smiled a broad smile as I went on to confess, "I fear you tapped the pubescent boy in me back there."

She put down her glass. "I'll never forget your generosity! Why are you like that? You're not guarded. Haven't you ever had your heart broken?"

I smiled enigmatically.

She looked deeply into my eyes. "You're an odd character, Dougay."

The meat platter, once again, was superb. After the plates were cleared away, I ordered us both another beer. When they were placed before us, Margarita leant forward, took hold of my hand and played meaningfully with my fingers.

Oh hell, I thought. *This feels like the grip of someone about to admit they're falling in love.*

"Dougay," she began, "I have one question."

"Go ahead," I said, looking into those big dark eyes.

"Where are you intending to meet Mary-Anne Walton?"

Chapter 15

I was overcome by a savage chest pain. I let go of Margarita's hand and sat back, trying to find a cohesive sentence. "Wo…What…Who?"

"You know who," Margarita said in a tone of voice I'd not heard before, her eyes not leaving mine.

I gathered myself. "Mary-Anne Walton is dead."

Margarita's expression did not change.

"How do you know about *her?* Who *are* you?" I stood. "Who are *you* to know of *her*? And *my* connection to her?"

"Please—sit down—I'll explain," whispered Margarita, not wishing to draw attention to us.

I was held there, unable to move, looking back at her. Those big brown eyes didn't have a skerrick of romance in them. They were cold and inquisitive. Becoming aware of my looming frame hovering over the table, and what the others in the restaurant may be thinking, I sat back down, still shaking, picking up my serviette and wiping beads of perspiration from my upper lip.

Margarita lowered her voice. "I'm CIA."

"Holy shit!" I whispered. "And you've been—following me?"

"Yes."

"All through Türkiye?"

"Yes."

"Wait a minute! You were hardly following me—for part of it, I took you with me!"

"You are a most convivial, trusting guide."

"And gullible! You took advantage of me. My good nature!"

"Yes," she said simply, adding, "It's my job." I stared back at her. "So, I repeat my question. Where is Mary-Anne Walton?"

"And I repeat my answer, Mary-Anne Walton is dead."

I couldn't contain myself any longer. I stood again. "Margarita, you used me—mistakenly—but you've still used me."

"I apologise for that," she said, sounding honest, though I didn't believe her. Whoever believes what the CIA tells them? Though in reality, they'd never told *me* anything before this.

"Margarita—this is my last night in Türkiye and I—foolishly—was going to invite you back to my room, if you wish to, to…you know. To be honest, I was falling for you. In Canakkale, I lay awake at night thinking of you. I'll pay this bill as promised. I'm *honest* that way. Have a good evening."

I headed to the bar, paid the father, shook his hand and the hand of his son, and bid them farewell, wishing them a safe and fulfilling life. I didn't look back at Margarita, the CIA agent. I left the restaurant and was thankful that the dolmus arrived at the stop at the same time I did. At the hotel, I didn't drop into the twelfth floor and in anger beat up her CIA partner—that shit head Miguel. Though I sure felt like it.

*

I was stretched out on my bed, a lot calmer now, thinking of how I fell on the ferry's steps, how Margarita had been right there behind me, and how she ingratiated herself. I recalled her sticking the elastoplast on my shin, her bringing me the cold beer into the water below, her big dark smiling eyes, and her running across the hot sand, satisfying every boyish fantasy I'd ever had.

There was a knock at the door. I opened it.

Margarita stood there. "May I come in?" She asked.

I leant across the doorway, barring her entry. "Are you wearing a wire?"

She laughed. "No."

"I don't believe you," I said, cautiously.

She shrugged that off. She gently laid her hand on my shoulder, appealing to my earlier feelings for her. I resisted, though not for long.

"If you come in here," I began, "you will take two steps into the room and then you'll stop. I will then close the door behind you. Once closed, you will remove all your clothing so I can see if you're wearing a wire or not."

"In my hand bag, I have latex gloves for any further inspection you may be contemplating," she teased. "Remember, I'm the professional in the room when it comes to body searches."

She pushed by me and stopped two paces in. I closed the door. Margarita wasn't wearing a wire!

*

"So, because of what you've confessed, I gather Miguel is not really your brother," I said to Margarita sometime later, a cool ocean breeze wafting the curtains over my balcony door.

"No, he isn't," she admitted. "Not even a distant cousin."

"Why would the CIA be interested in following *me*? I'm no one. I'm merely on holiday, as you have seen. I'm hardly a threat to US security."

"Okay, I confess. This assignment is very bottom-of-the-barrel stuff. Miguel doesn't believe he deserves this demotion. He's not usually this ornery."

"You'd better explain."

"Three weeks back, at a mandatory training course, a fellow officer teased him about his 'overprotective' attitude towards the women in the program. Miguel can be a bit of a white knight when it comes to protecting women's reputations."

"Yours?"

Margarita paused a moment. "Yes," she admitted. "This fellow male officer was making disparaging sexist comments about me. Miguel lost his temper and hit him—a clean clip on the jaw. Luckily, they were both unarmed at the time and other officers were there to separate them."

"So, for his sins, Miguel has had to tail me through Türkiye?"

"Yes."

"And why are you here? Did you sin as well?"

"I'm new to the game. Everyone has to start at the bottom. This is my first overseas assignment. Just quietly, we are gathering *intel* for the Justice Department."

"So, for Miguel, I'm seen as his demotion. I gather he doesn't like slumming, eh?"

"No."

"What about you?"

"Well, I'm pleasantly surprised at what I've managed to pick up in the gutter."

Later in the dark, I could feel Margarita beginning to wake, the pace of her rhythmic breathing altering.

"Where were you intending to follow me to?" I asked her. "Back to Nice?"

"Only as far as Rome," she confessed.

"So, you know my entire itinerary?" She didn't answer. "Are we, all three, on the morning ferry to Samos?"

"Yes."

I rolled onto my side, giving her my back. Frankly, I couldn't get all this CIA stuff out of my head. I again heard Pierre Legrande ask me, *is that CIA man following me or you?* No matter what, I had to admit being with Margarita was scary fun.

After a time, I managed to fall asleep. When I woke in the morning, she was gone. *Aren't all beautiful women with whom I get involved?*

Chapter 16

I checked out of the hotel with plenty of time to catch the dolmus down to the ferry terminal. Wandering mindlessly through customs, I thanked the lady when she stamped my passport and smiled at the security guy as he patted me down and ran a scanner up between my legs.

"Careful, I've valuables in there," I said cheekily, not expecting him to understand English.

"As we all do, sir," he replied. I laughed. "Have a nice day," he offered.

"Likewise, Monsieur."

I dragged my suitcase to the ferry. The gangplank was down so I drifted on and took the stairs up to the seat at the stern of the boat where I'd sat on the way over. *Was it only last week Margarita bandaged my leg here?*

People arrived in dribs and drabs. Yootha came down the dock dragging her suitcase, sunglasses covering whatever emotion she was feeling. Looking about, she didn't see me on the ferry's top deck. She remained on the dock, waiting.

Margarita had been honest when she said that she and Miguel would be on the morning ferry. She climbed the stairs up to the back deck. As she emerged, I smiled and beckoned her to sit with me. Miguel followed her up. He saw me and made out the sun was too bright, before turning around and bumping into a woman carrying a baby. He excused himself as he went down into the covered seating below.

"Well, here we are once again," Margarita said, placing her hands on her knees.

"Yes, and it's a very pleasant position to be in. Though compared to last night …"

"Shh—there's no need to be falsely friendly now that I've confessed everything to you."

"I'm not being false. I'm very happy having you sit next to me." I took her hand and squeezed it. She smiled. I think it was the woman who smiled, not the undercover operative.

Below, Yootha was still standing down on the dock. *She's going to miss the ferry,* I thought. A boat hand indicated for her to get on board. He lifted the thick mooring rope from around the bollard. She picked up her suitcase and stepped towards the gangplank. Suddenly there was a shouted: *Yootha!* from the immigration office. Cyril ran towards her dragging his suitcase. They fell into each other's arms, gathered themselves and rushed onto the ferry. I wondered if Desli was happier now she had the entire cabin to herself.

I said nothing to Margarita concerning the resolution of the love affair, instead settling back. After a short while of letting the sun soak in, I began to wonder what Miguel was doing down below amongst the screaming children and unconcerned parents. *Plotting,* I thought, *plotting my demise—somehow, somewhere—bringing me down to earth with a bang.* I just hoped the bang wasn't going to come from a revolver in the form of an accidental bullet to the head.

The idling engines stirred and the ferry eased out of the harbour, dwarfed once again by the luxurious cruise vessels. I wondered which one Big Barry was on singing his songs to annoyed passengers, and I hoped Pierre, back in Nice, wouldn't be too disappointed that I didn't find a rich American divorcée to rope me, hog tie me, and ship me off to Arizona.

"Dougay…" Margarita started.

"Is this about you-know-who?" I leant in and whispered, *"Elle est morte."*

Pulling down my straw hat over my dark glasses, I pretended to nod off. I didn't. I kept a watchful eye on the set of stairs in front of me in case Miguel decided to make his play and charge up, heaving me over the side to swim my way back to Greece.

Sometime later, the ferry slowed and we entered Samos Harbour. Keeping my distance, I followed Margarita and Miguel through immigration and customs and dragged my bag across the street to the Samos Hotel opposite. In the foyer, Miguel came up to me. I tensed. He whispered, "Don't push your luck. Last night was a mistake on her part. If you touch Margarita again, I'll beat the shit out of you."

"I don't doubt it," I said. "You have an advantage over me. As you now realise, after last night, I'm a lover, not a fighter." I stepped back, out of his arm's reach, hoping my barb had hit home but wary all the same in case he was intending to make good his threat.

Margarita stepped into me, smiling, extending her hand. I took it gently. "It's been lovely knowing you, Dougay. My brother and I could not have had such a wonderful time without you. May memories of Gallipoli stay with you forever."

She hasn't told Miguel I know they're CIA! She's still peddling the ruse that they are brother and sister. What a girl! Maybe she did care for me, after all. Maybe that phone number she'd written on the Türkish note was real. Maybe her visit to my room last night was not a last desperate attempt to have me unwittingly answer her persistent question.

I held back, letting them check-in. I noticed the desk clerk handed them *separate* room keys. *There's still hope, Dougay!* They walked to the elevator, leaving me behind in the foyer. *Ah well, hope can easily evaporate!*

Margarita turned back, crossed to me and formally extended her hand once more. "*Au revoir*, Dougay. It's been nice."

Nice? Cut your losses, Dougay, and move on.

Margarita left in my palm a red ten Türkish lira note. On it she'd scrawled: *Room 216.*

*

The next morning, Margarita and Miguel were on the same flight as me from Samos to Athens. Unlike on the way over, we took separate cabs to the airport because I didn't need any shit from Miguel, not yet anyway. I was intending to push his buttons a little later in the day.

At Athens airport, the same bus driver sped us across the tarmac to the terminal. My baggage had been checked through to Rome, so I found a plastic coffee and croissant. I waited until the flight was called, and let some eager beavers rush to line up and show their boarding passes.

I stood as Miguel moved to the gate. Walking by him, I whispered in my poor American accent, "Gee pal, your sister's great in the sack!"

Gallantly protecting Margarita's honour, Miguel spun me and threw the punch he'd been bottling up. I managed to move my head, the blow glancing my cheek though still knocking me forward. It had the power and timing of a punch thrown by a trained CIA agent and not your average overly outraged brother. I didn't resist the fall. I landed on a woman's knees and then onto her carry-on luggage, my coffee spilling everywhere, though thankfully not on her. She screamed in fright. Her husband protested in alarm.

I didn't try to get up. I tensed my stomach muscles. On cue, Miguel let fly with a kick to the guts. As his foot connected, I bent inwards, riding the impact. I stayed down. I had to; the kick hurt!

There was pandemonium around me now. Greek voices were shouting and two armed airport police officers rushed forward and grabbed Miguel. He protested in English; however, the Greek voices around me were drowning him out, no doubt explaining how I was attacked for no apparent reason. The two uniformed officers dragged Miguel off. As I staggered to my feet, apologising to those around me, I heard him shout to Margarita, "Wait for me in Rome! Wait for me in Rome!"

*

On the flight to Rome, I left my seat down back near the toilets and headed to the pointy end of the plane. I found Margarita seated in Business Class. "Is this seat vacant?" I asked her.

She looked up at me and smilingly said, "You know it is."

I sat in the seat which had been reserved for Miguel. I smiled, lecherously. "So," I began, "do you happen to have a hotel room in Rome?"

"No," she replied, "I was hoping you'd have booked a double."

I patted her knee as if consoling a child. "Stick with me, kid," I began, in a terribly poor imitation of Bogart, "when in Rome, I'll show you the ruins."

She looked me squarely in the eyes. "After the last two nights with you—I've already seen the ruins."

*

In the morning, after a wonderful evening in Rome, taking in the moonlit sites with my gorgeous companion, I bid farewell to Margarita. *"Au revoir, mate!"* I whispered as I kissed her.

Did I want to see her again? The woman, yes, though not the agent. Can an ordinary bloke in France have a worthwhile relationship with an extraordinary CIA operative based in the USA and travelling the globe? I don't think so.

Once the flight from Rome to Nice took to the air, I finally felt completely relaxed. I had seen what I wanted to see and had done what I needed to get done.

Thank you, Madame Legrande, for suggesting I make the trip.

I recalled the fortuitous moment I tripped and banged my shin on the Samos/Kusadasi Ferry. Such luck! I couldn't have arranged it any better. To think, unbeknownst to me, Margarita Gomez, at that moment was right behind me, on hand to notice the accidental fall and to help me bandage my cut shin. You cannot fake a bleed. It helped the pain that she was so easy on the eye.

My shin became the ideal hiding place for Pierre's small card. Margarita had put the original plaster there, and all I had to do was place the card on that and add a clumsily cut piece of plaster over the top of it, the rougher looking the better, to cover it and to keep it in place. What Margarita so desperately wished to find out was always there in front of her eyes.

I recognised that voice, and felt the thrill of it, the moment I heard her explaining about Marc Antony rushing up the steps at the library in Ephesus. My heart skipped a beat when she stumbled and held onto my shoulder for support.

Later in the day, I was thrilled to find her alone, eating her lunch in the empty sun-baked seats of the ancient theatre. At the time, I had wondered from where she'd managed to find that red umbrella.

I climbed down, resting on the row of seating along from her, pretending to scratch my wound, in reality removing the card from its hiding place between the two strips of plaster on my shin.

"*Bonjour*, Dougay," she whispered.

"*Bonjour* Mary-Anne," I replied, just as quietly. "*Ca va?*"

I asked her to take a photograph of me, and I passed her my phone, covering the tiny card Pierre had given me. She took my phone and pocketed the card. I stood down two rows and asked if she could include the background, in particular the two Americans. She could see Margarita and her 'brother' Miguel waiting on the stage like ancient Greek actor-slaves who'd forgotten their exit cue.

"Those two are CIA or Justice Department or State Department, or whatever," I said. "Be very careful."

"Yes," said Mary-Anne. "They walk as if they still have guns on their hips."

She passed me back my phone and I made a gesture of receiving it with thanks. I glanced fleetingly up into her beautiful eyes, as it was all I could afford to do. It was a glance which would have to last me a lifetime.

"Take care, Mary-Anne. Live a happy and full life. Thank you for the apartment. I can never repay you."

"You just have," she said, putting Pierre's card into her carry bag.

"I loved you, Mary-Anne Walton," I managed to say before I had to contain tears.

"And I loved you, Dougay Roberre."

Hastily wiping away tears with the back of my left hand, I stepped down, over the ancient stone seating to the American operatives. I did not look back to Mary-Anne.

The air hostess placed my beer in front of me, breaking my reverie. I thanked her as she poured it.

I smiled at the memory of what I'd said to Margarita and Miguel. *Are you two following me?*

I eased back my chair and sipped my drink.

Here's to the memory of a great holiday! I recalled Margarita allowing me to 'frisk' her, searching for a hidden wire. I laughed. *It's not every person in the world can say they've screwed the CIA!*

Chapter 17

In the taxi from Nice Airport, I was lost in the sweet thoughts of Margarita Gomez, though not for long. My mobile rang wiping away that delightful image of her standing on her hotel balcony waving a beer bottle at me in the water below!

"Have you landed, yet?"

"Remy, I'm in the cab heading home. Why?"

"Get over here!" he shouted.

"Where are you?" I asked, taken aback by the ferociousness in his voice.

"The warehouse! Where else?" He hung up.

The taxi driver dropped me outside Remy's warehouse. I paid him and he drove away. Dragging my suitcase to the roller door, I banged on it. The single steel door opened. Remy did not enquire about my holiday. He merely flicked his head, indicating *Enter!*

I dragged my luggage past him into the darkened space, my eyes attempting to adjust. At Remy's desk sat a man. As I approached, he stood and turned with a reflexive shrug of the shoulders and a rapid shake of his head. Perhaps he needed to ease some muscles at the top of his spine or a physical mannerism had cemented itself into his body language over the years. Dark-haired, unshaven and my height, he was muscularly built. I figured the muscles had not come from a gym, but rather from working in a trade that demanded physicality. My eyes adjusted fully, and it dawned on me who he was.

What the hell is he doing here? I asked myself. It was Cecily's brother—Gunther Valleaux!

Remy slid a chair behind me and said, "Sit!" He pushed down on my shoulders. I sat faster than I'd intended.

"Four evenings ago," began Remy, pointing to Gunther, "I was set upon in the street by this man. Why? Why should a complete stranger decide to attack me in a darkened street?"

"Theft?" I offered, having no idea why Gunther should be here with Remy.

"He wasn't after money! Look at him. You recognise him?" Remy didn't wait for my reply. "After we'd exchanged a few blows and danced about each other, I finally shouted: *What's this all about?* He stopped swinging and told me that he'd seen my truck leaving the cemetery and that he has a friend in administration, which is how he tracked me down."

I turned to Cecily's brother. "Gunther," I began, "Cecily deserves some happiness. You can't suppress the feelings of a grown woman forever."

"What are you talking about?" Gunther asked, belligerently. I now understood why his sister needed to get away.

"Love will always find a way," I persisted. "Let your sister go."

Gunther looked back at me with scorn. He said deliberately, so I'd fully understand, "I-do-not-have-a-sister."

Oh dear! "Then who was the young woman at your mother's funeral?" I asked, puzzled.

"My mother? My mother died ten years ago."

Oh dear, oh dear! "Wasn't it the funeral of 'Madame Valleaux'?" I asked, remembering M'sieur Pom had found the details of her funeral in the newspaper for me.

"Madame Valleaux was my wife!"

Oh dear, oh dear, oh dear!

"Is the light in your tiny brain turning on yet?" Remy asked.

"I'm sorry, I've made a mistake. Please accept my sympathy for your loss, Gunther." He made no recognition of doing so. "If she's not your sister then who was the young woman with you at the funeral?"

"My dying wife's carer, her live-in nurse."

My mistakes were gathering baggage. "So, who's the young man you beat up?"

"Beat up? A young man?" He thought for a moment. "Oh, him! I don't know who he is. I came home early one day and I found this thief in the house going through things. I grabbed him. I hit him. I was angry! I've been through a lot lately." He smacked his clenched fist into the palm of his other hand as if remembering one of the blows he'd given Guy Franc. "He managed to run away."

What have you foolishly gone and done, Dougay? My friends were always telling me that one day my kindness would come back to bite me on the bum and today was the day! "So—those two—Cecily and Guy knew each other, then…"

"Yes, obviously," Gunther said sarcastically, pleased I was finally catching on. "Her name's not Cecily. It's Simone."

Dougay, you have been well and truly taken for a ride! "What have they stolen?" I asked, now knowing what they had been up to.

"A collection of jade. A complete set of chess pieces in a finely crafted wooden box."

"Have you reported the theft to the police?" I asked.

Gunther scoffed dismissively.

"So, Dougay," said Remy, "*you* have a job to do. *You* have to find the thieves. *You* have to return the jade chess set to its rightful owner."

"Just like that?" I queried, clicking my fingers once.

"It is the honourable thing to do!" stressed Remy. I knew it was; he didn't have to tell me. I just didn't know how I was going to go about it.

"Are you going to get it back or not?" Gunther asked, becoming frustrated with my inaction, his anger rising once more.

"If you don't find the jade," said Remy, "I'll beat you up for involving me in your act of stupidity. Then Gunther here will demand his retribution."

Remy began to tap his fingers. Gunther played with the ring on his left hand. I stood and began to pace. Sometimes I think better on my feet. This wasn't one of them. I turned back to Remy and Gunther, shrugging helplessly. "I know nothing about them!"

Gunther didn't like hearing that. "*Merde!*" he growled, menacingly.

"Dougay," began Remy, trying to sound calm and reasonable, "you have to redress Gunther's loss and inconvenience. It's time to begin. Do you know anything about this young man? Anything at all?"

I scratched my head. It was time to get Margarita and Türkiye completely out of my mind and replace those thoughts with coherent ones.

Gunther, seathing, spun the ring on his left hand. "Think!" he demanded.

I noticed that the head of his ring was a skull and crossbones. *A skull and crossbones? A pirate ring? Hasn't this man grown up yet?* I wondered. *Concentrate, Dougay!*

"Gunther, where did you find your wife's nurse?" I asked, clutching at the first straw which came my way. "Was it through a friend's recommendation? Or through a hospital? Or an agency?"

"An agency." Gunther reached into his wallet, removed a business card and thrust it at me. I made out I was pleased to receive it. The card read: *Twilight Aged Services. Monsieur and Madame Pallent. Your loved one remains loved in our care.*

"May I keep this?" I asked Gunther.

"Why should I want it back?" He questioned sarcastically. "My wife no longer needs their services."

"For how long had she been with you, this 'Cecily' or 'Simone'?"

Gunther thought a moment, calculating. "Only two months. My wife deteriorated quite quickly."

"And you approached the aged care providers? They didn't come to you?"

"Yes, I called them."

"When Simone lived with you, was there anything peculiar or out of the ordinary about her?"

Gunther shook his head. "No, nothing. I rarely saw her. She spent her time with my wife, prepared her food and went to bed early. Most nights, when I'd get home from work, I ate their leftovers alone at the table. There was no communication between Simone and me."

"Did she have visitors?"

"No."

"Did she go out in the evenings?"

"She spent Saturday night out and returned by breakfast on Sunday. Oh, she liked a walk occasionally in the early morning before my wife had woken."

I remembered seeing Simone and Guy on the promenade after I'd taken an early morning swim. They'd been plotting alright and not their romantic life together!

"So, that's it?" I asked.

"Are you doubting me?" Gunther was becoming irritated with me once more. Maybe he didn't like being questioned—by anyone, and not specifically me. However, questions were all I had at the moment because I sure didn't have any answers.

"No, I'm not doubting you," I admitted. "Have there been any odd phone calls? Or tradesmen coming to the door?"

"Not when I was home." His tone turned to sarcasm. "How would I possibly know when I wasn't at home?"

I ignored the jibe. "This young man called himself 'Guy Franc'. Had you ever seen him in the street? Outside your house, casing the place? Maybe observing you leave home for work?"

"No. He didn't need to. Simone lived with us. She'd have searched the house thoroughly during the past two months. I don't have much of value. Everything I have is tied up in my business. This chess set is very sentimental to me. It came from my wife's father and his father before that."

The chess set had obviously been in Cecily's suitcase, the one Guy had with him, the heavy one I'd lifted into Jules' car. *I bet that key Guy Franc gave me was a fake as well! Oh boy, did that young man play you, Dougay!*

Gunther stood quickly, again shrugging his shoulders and rapidly twitching his head.

"Anything else?" I asked.

"Yes," the strongly built man replied, fiddling with his pirate ring. "Get back my jade chess set. You have until the weekend. Then I'll be coming for you." I didn't doubt that for a second.

He began to leave. At the door, he turned back and spat, "Idiot, meddlesome idiot!"

Remy agreed. And to be honest, so did I.

*

Louise was at home when I arrived back at Avenue Auber. She ran from her bedroom and hugged me. If only I wasn't so distracted, I'd have fully appreciated the moment.

"Louise, you remember that young man who was beaten up? I helped him at the café?"

"What?" She asked surprised. "That's how you greet me after your holiday?"

"Sorry, but I need to ask you something."

She ignored me and made a point of looking out the door to the elevator. "Where's the rich American widow?"

"There were far too many to choose from. I couldn't decide between an inheritance of gold or oil."

She laughed. "You didn't leave behind your questionable sense of humour."

I closed the door and carried my luggage towards my bedroom. "Louise, seriously, do you remember him? The young man who'd been beaten up?"

"Of course."

"You said he'd been staying at the hostel?"

"Yes, he had. What's this about, Dougay?"

Where was I going to start? I couldn't tell her everything I'd learnt since arriving back in Nice. Louise looked up to me. I couldn't dent her admiration of me.

"Have you messed up, again, Dougay?"

I nodded I had. "It turns out he's stolen something from a friend. Come with me to that hostel, please, Louise. I need you to ask some questions."

*

I let Louise go into the hostel alone. I didn't want the receptionist checking me out, a forty-two-year-old man walking into a doss house with a twenty-year-old woman. Knowing my luck, the manager would call the cops!

Louise felt the reason for enquiring about Guy Franc, had to be ordinary. "After all, no one staying in a hostel is secretly hiding the plans for a sea invasion of Monaco!"

"You're correct. Tell them you lent Guy some personal photos and you want them back."

It was twenty minutes before Louise came out. We headed to a café down the street. I ordered two coffees.

"I asked the sleazy man on the desk if he'd seen Guy Frank around lately. He was most unhelpful. He wanted to see my ID. He wanted to know what I was *really* after. Did I owe the hostel money when I checked out? I gave up on him because a casual acquaintance walked in. According to her, Guy Franc is still around, but he only spends a night or two, until he disappears for a stretch. Though she hasn't seen him for a while."

The waitress brought over the coffee.

Louise took a sip. "Yuk! That coffee's not as nice as ours."

I took a sip; Louise was correct.

"Then the guy behind the desk at the hostel decided to add in his bit as well. He said that Guy's got a new girlfriend, a nurse and that I'd be hard-pressed to get back the photos. He leered at me and said to search porn sites on the internet!"

Nurse? Yes, Gunther had said she was a nurse.

I clicked my fingers. Milovic's sister-in-law, Ljuba, was a nurse at a psychiatric hospital up near the Chagall museum.

Come on, Dougay, you're supposed to be a wizard at joining the dots!

I wondered if Ljuba ever had any dealings with *Twilight Aged Services.*

"Maddie," said Louise, pushing the coffee to one side.

"Pardon?"

"Madeleine. She's a friend from my time at the hostel. I'm sure she went out once or twice with Guy Franc. Maybe she still has his number."

Louise stood and walked outside, mobile to her ear, nodding, laughing and catching up on old times. While she was at it, I hoped she wouldn't forget to catch up on present times. She hung up and fiddled with her phone. My mobile pinged. It was the contact number for Guy Frank!

Waving me goodbye, I mimed back: *Don't you want your coffee?*

Louise made a gagging gesture and shook her head. I waved, thanking her.

I went to tap Guy's number. *No! That's not a good idea, Dougay!* Instead, I forwarded it to Remy. After a moment, I tapped Remy's number.

"Remy—I've just sent you a mobile number. Your mate Electro, the guy who installed my television, is he any good at tracing?"

"You want to find out where the mobile is?"

"Yes."

"Is this the number of the thief?"

"Yes. If Electro can trace it, we can go give Guy Franc a visit in Montpellier and maybe wrap this up before Gunther's deadline."

"No. Electro can't do that. He's not a magician."

"Oh," I said disappointed. "Alright, time to think of other things."

"However, his wife, Madame Electro, is a civilian who works for the police in technical administration. I'm sure she can trace it. From memory, she works the night shift. Leave it with me."

Rather than wait all night for Madame Electro to put a trace on Guy's phone, that is if she could, I decided to follow a few more leads—though I hoped they weren't going to be of the dead-end variety.

Chapter 18

I pushed open the door to *Lefbvre and Massenet*, jewellers. The little bell above the door tinkled. The woman behind the counter looked up. "Oh hello—you've returned!"

"Yes," I replied, my most warming smile beginning to spread across my face. With people I like, I find it difficult to conceal my genuine feelings towards them. "Madame, would it be possible to have a quick word with Monsieur Antoine Massenet, please?"

"I'll see if he's free, Monsieur Roberre," she said, stepping into the room behind the counter. I glanced at the diamond engagement rings in the showcase. *No need to consider one of those*, I reminded myself.

Madame Massenet returned. "Come through," she beckoned.

I walked into the familiar room and held out my hand to the smiling jeweller. He took it.

"Dougay Roberre, welcome back." He beckoned me to sit, and after his wife had returned to the shopfront, asked, "You have more diamonds to sell?"

"No, unfortunately, I'm all out of diamonds."

"Ah," he shrugged, "the reality of life. Then, how may I be of assistance?"

"I have a friend who's been robbed."

Monsieur Massenet considered this. "And he hasn't reported it to the police?"

"No."

The old jeweller nodded sagely. "I run a respectable business, Dougay. I'm neither a suspect pawn broker nor a fence."

"I realise that, sir. I apologise for any offence given. It's a request I wish to ask and I know of nowhere else to ask it. Perhaps you could put the word out amongst your associates. I don't doubt that there is some sort of old boy network of jewellers out there."

"You make us sound as if we're a cartel, which is against the law."

"I didn't mean that, Monsieur. I apologise again."

He studied me for a moment, then dropped his voice and asked, "What has been stolen?"

"Jade," I said simply, not knowing if that was valuable or not.

He considered this. "Such an odd thing to steal—quite a specialist market—it's rather old fashioned, you know—it's not flashy."

"It may have been all there was of value in the house. My friend doesn't strike me as being an art connoisseur or collector."

"Mmm, jade. Some believe jade has soothing and calming properties."

I thought of Gunther. His jade chess set hadn't calmed him. Then again maybe his calmness disappeared with its theft.

Monsieur Massenet nodded sagely. "Jade symbolises nobility and wealth."

The Gunther I knew, whether calm or riled, didn't possess either of those qualities.

"*Imperial* jade is valuable. Is that what has been stolen?"

"I have no idea, Monsieur."

"Mmm," considered Monsieur Massenet again. "These days, thieves go for the flashy stuff. Men, who buy under the counter, or off the back of a truck, believe 'sparkles' will impress a woman. Jade has a sense of investment about it. No man wants to give a mistress the sense of the long term."

I moved him on. "The thief was only in his mid-twenties."

"You know the thief?" Monsieur Massenet asked in disbelief.

"Yes and no. I'd rather not go into too much detail, Monsieur Massenet. Let's just say I have exceedingly strong suspicions."

The old man accepted that. He began to think, tapping a finger on his desktop. No decision or advice was ever hurried by Monsieur Massenet.

"Was it a rush job?" He eventually asked. "A smash and grab? Do you know?"

"It was well thought out. He had knowledge of what was in the house. His girlfriend, also his accomplice, was a live-in aged care worker, so she had plenty of time to search the rooms. He had tried previously, though the owner came home early and gave him a thumping. When the young man finally stole the jade, the owner of the house was away at a funeral—the death of his wife—the woman nursed by the thief's accomplice."

"Where has ethical morality gone? You can't trust anyone these days." Monsieur Massenet slowly shook his head. "Jade," he considered yet again. "I wouldn't think there'd be a large market for this."

"The jade is in the form of a set of chess pieces."

"Mmm, that's an even smaller market."

"In a quality wooden case."

From inside his desk drawer, Monsieur Massenet took out a black address book. Inside it were hand written details. "Jade chess pieces being off loaded by a young man and woman—I wonder if they're in a hurry to sell."

"They were stolen about ten days ago."

"Then let's hope they think they've waited long enough for the heat to go out of the theft." He thought a moment more. "Peddling jade, I'm sure they won't slip under the radar. The problem is we'll only know about it depending upon the honesty of the jeweller they happen to approach. Not that any of my colleagues are not, you understand."

"They said they were heading to Montpellier, though now I think that could have been part of the ruse."

"Then let's check Montpellier first before we eliminate it."

He opened his directory to a page and ran his finger under a name scrawled there. "I'll ring this jeweller in Montpellier." He reached for his ornate landline. I sat back and waited.

There ensued a conversation in hushed tones. To my ears, some of it may have been spoken in shorthand of the trade. Monsieur Massenet bid his caller, *au revoir*, and hung up.

"No, there's nothing to report in Montpellier. And before you ask, my younger brother would not lie to me. He's heard nothing."

I nodded, just as I feared, a dead-end.

"How far afield do you think they'll travel to off-load the jade?" He asked.

"They used Nice as a base. They'd meet up on Saturday evening at a local youth hostel. Stay there cheaply. The young woman appears to have been employed by an aged service provider here in Nice."

"Leave it with me, Dougay. I'll call you, if and when I have anything."

"Also call me if you have nothing. At least I'll know that avenue is a dead-end." I stood to leave. "Have you heard from Audric?"

"Yes. He's settled into Paris. He has an apartment in the 9th arrondissement. He's happy. There's a woman."

"That's very pleasing to hear. Audric is one of nature's true gentlemen. Wish him well for me, please, Monsieur Massenet."

"Most certainly, Dougay."

"If you can help locate this jade chess set," I began, reaching for my wallet and dropping a hundred euros on his desk, "I'd be most grateful."

He handed me back the money. "Pay me only if my enquiries lead to a successful recovery. Then, I'll take only fifty."

"Thank you, Monsieur, there are so few honourable people left in this world."

"Honourable?" He queried, with a twinkle in his eye. "Well, I guess, one of us in the room may be."

*

I took out the business card Gunther had given me. *Twilight Aged Services.* I decided not to call, that it'd be better if I tried the personal touch. I walked beyond the Old Town towards the railway line on the eastern side of Nice. The office was in an ordinary apartment building. I rang the outside bell, was let into the foyer, and climbed the stairs to the first floor.

"Yes?" came a crackly woman's voice from the locked door's intercom.

"*Bonjour*, Madame, my name is Dougay Roberre. I wonder if I may have a word?"

The door was buzzed unlocked, and I pushed against it. Inside, I was met by a fiftyish-year-old woman, not overly dressed, oozing practicality. She adjusted the glasses on her nose so she could make a better assessment of the stranger before her.

"Madame Pallent. Would it be possible to speak with her, please?"

"You are, Monsieur," the woman replied as if she was of no great importance.

"Madame, I need your assistance."

"In what way? Do you need help with an aged parent?"

"No, Madame."

"Being a man, someone to clean your apartment once a week?"

"No, Madame. I was wondering if you have a Cecily or a Simone on your books?"

Madame Pallent studied me. "Monsieur, we are not a dating agency."

"No, I just need to know…"

"We are a reputable palliative care agency. Do you honestly believe that I would give you any details of people who work or do not work for us? You people are degenerates. *Au revoir!*"

*

I called Milovic and asked him to join me, after he'd finished driving his limousine for the day, at *Vlatava-Elbe*. "Oh, and bring Ljuba with you, please."

"Pasha may not allow her out, to go to a bar with you." How did I get such a reputation amongst my friends?

"Tell him, he can come also and I'll buy the drinks."

"We'll all be there!" gleefully exclaimed my Czech mate.

I hung up and phoned Jules St Croix.

"Ah, Dougay, you're still alive?" The private detective asked. "I thought Remy would have beaten the stuffing out of you by now."

"Still alive and trying to solve my embarrassing mistake."

"I told you one day your kindness would get you into…"

"Yes, yes, yes," I muttered, cutting short his looming lecture.

"So, enough chit-chat, eh?" He asked cheekily. He seriously added, "How may I be of service?"

"Did that young couple say anything in your car when you drove them to Marseille? Any hint as to where they might now be?"

"I had on headphones."

"Oh," I replied, disappointed.

"Special headphones," he whispered.

"What do you mean?" I asked, with aroused curiosity.

"Special Private Detective headphones—my own special design."

"You've lost me, Jules."

"They are ordinary headphones, but they have holes, the size of pin pricks in them so I can hear everything that's being said around me. Pretty clever, eh? While others assume I'm off in my own little dream world, listening to Couperin's Greatest Hits, I can focus in on what they're saying."

"That's cunning."

"Yes. I might try and sell the patent to the CIA."

A shiver ran through me. I didn't tell him I now have a contact there.

"Sly, deceitful and cunning," he reiterated. "That's why I'm the professional in this business and you're not. What do you wish to know about those two?"

"Whatever you can tell me."

"They were kissing and cuddling—all over each other in the back seat. Self-congratulations reigned supreme. They carried on as if they'd put something big over someone—and got away with it. I'm now assuming that someone was *you*."

"Yes, Jules, it was me."

"They were a little thrown at first on the journey heading towards Marseille as they were expecting to be on the train. I did manage to explain to them that from Marseille they'd have to make their own way to Montpellier. But guess what, Dougay?"

"What, Jules?"

"I got the distinct impression they were *not* interested in going to Montpellier."

"Really? Any idea where?"

"Yes, after a day or two in Marseille, back to Nice."

"Nice?" I questioned, not believing.

"Sure—when hiding from the police, hide in the shop next door to the police station."

"Thanks, Jules."

*

Milovic, Ulna, Pasha and Ljuba were waiting for me at *Vlatava-Elbe*. Milos, the owner of the bar, placed slivovitz on the table before us. I had intended to ask a few short, simple questions and then head off home. It now appeared I was in for a long night.

After they asked an endless array of questions about Türkiye, and we seemed to toast every Czech saint and noteworthy historical figure with a fresh shot of slivovitz, I finally managed to ask Ljuba, "Ever had dealings with *Twilight Aged Services?*"

"Yes," she said. "When Pasha and I first came to Nice, I applied for every nursing job I could find. I put my name down with them—amongst others."

"Did you work for them?"

"A couple of times—for day care only. Being married to Pasha, I didn't want to accept any live-in positions."

"Did they ever ask you to do anything—odd?"

"Odd?"

"Did they ask you to take particular notice of the layout of a person's house, or what valuable possessions they might have?"

"No, nothing like that. I found them to be excellent, honest employers. I only left them because I wanted more regular hours. They paid me what I was owed and on time."

It appeared that the Pallents of *Twilight Ages Services* weren't involved in the theft of the jade chess set. That meant I wasn't about to get caught up in some larger, organised gang of thieves. Two young thieves I think I can handle, but not an entrenched network of them.

I was now out of live threads. All I could do was wait and see if anyone would come through for me.

It had been a very long day. Was it only last night I kissed Margarita in front of the Trevi Fountain after tossing in a coin and playfully squeezing her ass in front of the Spanish Steps?

I bid my Czech mates *a bientot*, and walked my well-worn track back to Avenue Auber, hoping tomorrow, someone would know something.

Chapter 19

"Do you know what time this is?" I asked sleepily into my mobile.

"Yes, time to get up!" It was Remy.

"Why?" I did not feel like doing so because my hips felt nailed to my bed. Can you get jet lag flying from Rome to Nice?

"Madame Electro has come through for us. Well, for *you!*"

I climbed out of bed and headed to the bathroom, juggling the phone around my ear. "And?" I dropped the phone. I scrambled, picking it up and shouting at arm's length, "Go on! What did she find out?"

"That phone number is still in Nice!"

"Still in town!" I was now fully awake. *Unbelievable! Jules had been correct!* "Give me twenty minutes, I'll come to you," I said, trying to pull down my pyjama pants with one hand.

"No," he countered. "I'll give you ten minutes—be down stairs. I'll pick you up in the truck."

In under ten minutes, I crossed the foyer as M'sieur Pom emerged from his apartment, stretching.

"Wow!" he exclaimed. "The early bird is off for his worm!"

I approached him, and being euphoric about finding the whereabouts of the two thieves, leant across his desk faking a big sloppy kiss! "Good morning!" I tugged playfully at his cheek.

"Yuk!" he spluttered and coughed, grotesquely. As I headed to the door, he called after me, "Did you need the first-aid kit?"

"More than you'll ever know!"

"Well then, do you think I could have it back?"

Remy was outside in his truck, one wheel up on the footpath. As I climbed up, he turned over the engine and we headed off.

"Where are we going?" I asked him. "Where are they hanging out?"

"The port area."

A minute later, Remy's mobile rang. He reached awkwardly into his pocket and handing it to me, said, "Answer that, will you."

"Hello? Remy Didion's phone."

"Put it on speaker!" Remy insisted. I did.

"Remy, the phone is moving," whispered Madame Electro, surreptitiously. "It's leaving the port area."

"Out of town?" Remy asked.

"It's too early to say. All I know is the signal is moving."

"Okay, Madame, call me back when you have a better idea."

"Will do, Remy." She hung up.

Remy pulled over and turned off the engine. We sat and waited. It was all we could do. He looked over to me and sniffed exaggeratedly. "Did you have a shower before you left?" I let his comment lie in the dust of dry humour where it belonged.

My mobile rang. It was the jeweller, Monsieur Massenet. "Sorry for ringing so early," he apologised, "I thought you'd want to know."

"That's okay, Monsieur, what do you have for me?"

I flicked my mobile to speaker mode.

"Late last night I got a call back from a colleague in Arles. A young woman came into his shop just before closing time with one piece of a jade chess set. She asked the usual questions. Is it valuable? How much for the complete set? My colleague said he was interested, but he'd need to see the complete set before giving an evaluation. She said she'd come back tomorrow, which is today when she would show him the set. She said she'd return in the late afternoon."

"Monsieur Massenet, you're a marvel! Thank you. What's the address?"

"I'll text you all the details." He hung up. I turned to Remy. "Come on, we're off to Arles."

Remy crunched the gears getting the truck into first.

"I could have done that," I said. "I thought you said you knew the subtleties of 'my old girl'?"

Holding firmly onto the steering wheel, Remy let out the clutch quickly. His truck lurched forward, tossing me back against the seat. Remy then braked savagely, and threw me forward, my hands stopping me from hitting the dashboard.

"My old girl seems to have a mind of her own this morning," he laughed.

Several minutes later, as we were heading to the entry for the E80, Madame Electro called back. "Remy! It's heading out of town!" I think she was up for the chase as well.

"Thank you, Madame! We think we know where it's going," Remy shouted above the engine noise. "When do you finish work?"

"In an hour. I can keep you posted on any changes until then."

"Madame, we think it's going to Arles," I explained. "Only ring back if it *doesn't* appear to be doing that."

"Will do!"

*

Thirty minutes down the E80 heading west, I was looking across Remy, when I suddenly ducked down below the window.

"What are you doing?" He asked, surprised.

"That's him! That grey car there, on your left."

Remy looked at the car out in the far lane, overtaking us. "Simple," he said. "I'll follow him."

"No need," I cautioned. "Let them come to us later this afternoon like we've planned, remember? We don't want to spook them."

"I suppose you're right," he begrudgingly admitted.

"Less speed, more haste," I reminded him.

Remy turned his head slowly to me and asked with false condescension, "From where do you pick up that verbal nonsense?"

*

The jewellery shop in Arles was located in the maze of streets beneath the amphitheatre, in from the old Roman gate, near the Baths of Constantine. Remy parked the truck under the flyover and we walked. Luckily, he knew where we were going, for I had no idea.

The jeweller was Monsieur Yves Ballant. According to Monsieur Massenet, they were more than colleagues; they were old friends, having dated the same girl when they were teenagers. I hoped neither held a grudge because I needed this man's assistance.

129

A tastefully painted sign above the door read: *Ballant et Ballant—Jewellers to the trade.*

It was a little before 3 p.m. Hopefully, the young thieves hadn't panicked and decided to rush here to complete the transaction early and get out of town as fast as they could.

Pushing open the door I carefully stepped inside.

"Dougay Roberre?" An old voice enquired from the gloom.

"Monsieur Ballant, old time friend of Monsieur Massenet of Nice?"

The jeweller appeared into the light, cast through the window in the door. "What was the girl's name?" He asked. This was our pre-arranged greeting.

"Jeanne," I replied. "Monsieur Massenet said that her hair was blonde and long, and her legs…"

"Yes, there's no need to remind me," muttered Monsieur Ballant. "My old friend loves teasing, even of events that are best described as 'Ancient History'." He extended his hand and I shook it. "Call me 'Yves'." He looked past me. "That man outside," he began to ask nervously, "he looks suspicious. Do you know him?"

I turned. "Yes, sadly, I do. He's with me."

"On closer look, he seems familiar."

"He was once a fighter—Remy Didion."

"Remy Didion? I saw him fight his last fight!" The old jeweller was becoming excited. "I lost two hundred euros on him!"

"Apparently, he broke his hand."

"He broke my wallet!"

I thought Monsieur Ballant was going to share a moment of philosophic insight with me. You know, *don't throw away your hard-earned money on sporting contests,* or *gambling is an idiot's game.* No, Monsieur Ballant went outside onto the narrow footpath and shook Remy's hand! They stayed out there conversing like old friends.

I knocked on the inside of the open door to get their attention. Coming back in, Monsieur Ballant said, "The inspection is for four forty-five and it will not be here. She is suspicious, which is natural."

"Where will it be?" Remy asked of his new 'long-lost friend'.

"I do not know—yet. She is to call with the location of the meeting place. Do you know Arles, Monsieur Roberre?"

"No," I said.

"He knows nothing of France," said Remy, dismissively. "He grew up with the kangaroos." He pointed to the floor. "Down there!" He laughed at his poor gag. "I know Arles. I once fought here."

"Yes," said the jeweller. "It was the scene of a famous victory. You took Tiger Thurian in the fifth—a clean punch to the jaw. He went down for the count if I remember correctly."

"You do," said Remy simply, slightly embarrassed. He'd never spoken to me in depth of his pugilistic career.

"So, gentlemen, all we can do is wait for her to make contact. Leave me your mobile number and I'll call you when she phones. Remy, may I suggest that you take Monsieur Roberre for a walking tour of Arles, up around the amphitheatre."

We bid Monsieur Ballant *adieu* and set off. Around a corner, tourists were taking photographs of a café. I stopped and held Remy by the arm.

"Why are tourists taking selfies in front of that building?"

"Some painter made it famous."

I read a nearby plaque. "Some painter? It was Van Gogh! Vincent Van Gogh!"

"Yes, that's him." Remy walked off and I followed, heading up the hill.

At the amphitheatre, we manoeuvred our way past groups of tourists standing and sitting on the outside steps, catching some of the little shade the ancient stone building managed to spread on the ground ahead of us. I paid our admittance, and following the sign-posted arrows, we climbed and sat up high in the bleachers. It immediately reminded me of the theatre in Ephesus though the seating here had been restored and the entrances updated.

"They hold bullfights here," Remy informed me.

I shuddered. "I detest bullfights. I want the bull to win. I will always support the underdog."

"Bulls, not dogs," Remy said, dryly.

I gave him a sideways glance, not deigning to comment.

"Here in Provence, we French love the bull. In Spain, they do not. That is why they kill the bull. Here our bulls are heroes. They are adored and live long lives. Some even take on legendary status and are given a hero's farewell upon retirement."

My mobile rang. It was Monsieur Ballant.

"*Alyscamps*," he said. "The old Roman cemetery and medieval church."

"Repeat that, please, Monsieur," I said, handing the phone to Remy, who listened attentively, nodded, and finally replied, "We can walk there. You take a cab, Monsieur Ballant. Dougay will pay."

We headed up the steep rise around the amphitheatre and the tourist shops. At the top of the rise, with the old Roman Theatre on our right, we headed downhill through a park, left at a major street, then right at traffic lights and further downhill. A while later we were at the entrance to *Alyscamps*. Waiting for Monsieur Ballant, I read the sign out front in depth, as I was curious about what was inside.

A taxi pulled up next to the small parking lot opposite. Remy crossed and held open the door while Monsieur Ballant climbed out. Remy deliberately waved me over to pay the driver. As if I was going to renege on that! Inside the front gate of the ancient burial ground, I paid for three entry tickets.

A tree-lined path with scattered sarcophagi led to a twelfth-century church far down the end. Our walk from the gate was almost funereal. A couple of departing tourists passed and underneath our feet, the crunch of small gravel stones was the only sound. Before we reached the end of the path, we stopped and stood in the shade of a tree. The late afternoon sun was very warm.

"The meeting is to be inside the church," explained Monsieur Ballant, pointing ahead to the far end, "not in any of the small chapels off to the side on the way down. On the phone, she made sure I understood that."

Remy, looking about said, "There's a fence all the way around this site. They won't be easily running away. I'll wait up by the entrance. They have to come out the way they came in." He walked away. He stopped and turned back, saying pointedly to me, "Don't worry. I'll keep my head down."

Monsieur Ballant and I sat down by the church in the shade and waited.

*

At four-thirty, we walked into the church and waited inside in the dark. The corner we stood at had liberal droppings of bird shit on the ground. A lone motley pigeon fluttered above, flying from one cornice to another. To relieve the wait, I walked down the steps into the crypt; however, I soon walked back up again. I don't like dwelling too long in crypts, in case I forget to leave! By five o'clock, the woman had not arrived.

"She's not coming," said Monsieur Ballant, disappointedly. *He* was disappointed!

We waited in there a further twenty minutes, the lone pigeon finally settling on a spot for the evening. Accepting Guy's and Cecily's non-show, we reluctantly walked slowly from the church into the bright light, shielding our eyes.

There was a kerfuffle up ahead, a rapid shuffle of feet in the gravel. The young thieves had recognised me and turned, running off. I sprinted after them.

Panicking in flight, they bumped into a distracted tourist taking a photograph of his wife lying prone on a stone burial slab, pretending she was a sacrificial virgin. It required a lot of pretending. "Hey!" the American man shouted at them. "God damn it!"

The thieves ran out of the cemetery and onto the street heading uphill. Where was Remy? He'd promised he'd be waiting by the entrance gate. "Remy?" I shouted.

The young man, carrying the chess set, was fit. The weight of the jade wasn't slowing him down. I calculated that if the hill levelled out, I might be able to run down Simone inside a hundred metres.

Up ahead they jumped into that grey car I'd seen pass us on the highway. Guy turned over the ignition and the car hopped forward. The left rear tyre was flat! Then Remy was there, opening the driver's door and dragging Guy out onto the roadway. His kneecap slammed a savage 'hello' into the young man's guts, where Gunther had greeted him two weeks earlier.

I ran to the car's passenger door, flung it open and grabbed at the chess set being clutched by Simone. She tugged against me. Then she leant forward and bit my hand. I hate hitting women!

"Sorry, Simone," I said after I chopped her arm. She screamed as if I'd cut her throat! I grabbed the chess set and lifted it up onto the roof of the car to check that everything was intact.

It was certainly an impressive set. As Gunther had said, the pieces were inside a fine-crafted wooden box, with heavy felt lining keeping the individual pieces securely in place. To play the game you inverted the box, for built into its base was the black and white chequered board. The pieces were all accounted for.

I heard Guy protesting until Remy sunk his fist into his midriff again. Then I heard him spluttering for air.

Simone was now out of the car and scratching at me. She gashed my face! I reached out and held her by the throat.

"Stop!" I shouted. "Stop!" She calmed a little. I relaxed my grip.

She let fly with another savage scratch accompanied by, "You dumb useless fucking asshole!"

"That's hardly a character reference!"

She lashed out at me again.

I hate slapping women in the face!

I also hate their howling scream when I do!

Remy and I held them there in the gutter until they calmed.

Monsieur Ballant, out of breath, ambled up from the old cemetery's entrance. He passed an assessor's eye over the jade.

"Is it Imperial Jade?" I asked.

The jeweller removed one of the Queens, felt its weight and turned it over. "No. Its sentimental value far outweighs its monetary value."

I took a hundred euros out of my wallet and handed it to Monsieur Ballant. Ignoring the two on the ground, he accepted the money, thanked me, wished Remy well and strolled off.

Chapter 20

"One day we should spend more time in Arles. It seems to be a beautiful old town," I said to Remy as we left our car park under the flyover. I touched the sides of my face delicately, where Simone had scratched me. Opening the truck's glove box, I found a half roll of toilet paper and dabbed away the blood.

"You're hardly recognisable," said Remy. "You should thank her. She's scratched off the ugly bits."

The jade chess set sat safely, nursed in my arms, clutched to my chest, like the time I carried Audric's diamonds home from *Gare de Nice*. After Remy cursed several times while trying to find the entrance to the flyover, we headed home, the evening light streaking the roadway. I rubbed my bitten hand.

"I was worried back there," confessed Remy.

"About?"

"I thought you might offer those thieves a job!"

"They are not Louise. I'd never be able to trust them. I'm going to need time to recover. My sense of decency and belief in my fellow human being has taken a battering lately."

"Well, I hope, at last, you've learnt your lesson."

"I had no idea where you'd gotten to," I confessed. "I thought they were going to get away—simply drive off."

"Have I ever let you down?"

I didn't answer that, only giving him a prolonged sideways glance.

"When I was waiting at the entrance, I saw them drive past. I walked after them and watched where they parked. Then, when they left to bring the chess set to the cemetery, I let down the tyre. No matter what happened with you and Yves, they had to come back for the car."

I squeezed the chess set tighter with my left arm and found my mobile. I called Gunther.

"Yes? What is it?" He answered, belligerently.

"Dougay here. Gunther, I have good news for you. I have your chest set."

"About time!" Did he sound relieved, thankful? I couldn't tell.

"Tonight? Or tomorrow?" I asked him. "When would you like us to drop it around?"

"Tonight," he said emphatically and hung up.

"He's not very talkative," I joked. "You'd think he'd be at least a little pleased."

"I need petrol," replied Remy.

*

I paid for Remy's full tank of petrol. He turned over the engine of the old truck and we set off again.

"You're holding that chess set as if it were a baby!" He laughed, looking across at me, trying to tug the chess set from my grasp.

"Look out!" I screamed. The truck hit the speed hump and bounced us, even though we were both strapped in. Belatedly, Remy braked savagely.

"What's that?" He asked.

"A speed hump!"

"No, what's *that*?" He pointed at my chest. "There's a drawer at the base of the chess set!"

I looked down. A thin compartment between the chess board and the box containing the chess pieces had sprung open. Inside there was a piece of paper. Taking it out I unfolded it and immediately recognised the word: *CIH-D'AZ*.

"Holy *Merde*!" I instinctively exclaimed. "Drive on, Remy," I instructed, holding the letter out for him to see. "This name here—I know it."

"What name?" Remy asked, sensibly refusing to take his eyes off the road ahead.

"This company name or whatever—*CIH-D'AZ*. Before I went to Türkiye, Francine's law office was broken into. A letter from a file marked: *CIH-D'AZ* was stolen. I think this is that letter."

"Read it out," ordered Remy, as he turned the truck onto the highway. "I love secret love letters." Then he laughed. "You won't be able to. You can't read French!"

"I can read enough to make sense of this," I said, carefully placing the chess set at my feet. I studied the piece of paper. "It's no love letter. It's an agreement between several signatories. Holy *Merde!*"

"What? What is it now?"

"I recognise some names."

"Read the whole thing, the best you can. Start at the beginning."

I held the letter to my chest like I'd held the chess set, fearing I was about to reveal something earth-shattering.

"Remy, just *who* is Gunther Valleaux?"

"The guy who owns the chess set."

"Apart from that! Who is he *really*? Why would he have this document? Why would he steal it from Francine's office? How did he know it was there? Why would he store it in this secret compartment? What connection does he have to this letter?"

"So many questions," muttered Remy, sardonically, "so little time."

"What do we know about him?"

"Search the internet. See what turns up."

I let the agreement lie on my chest as I took out my phone and did as Remy suggested. I sifted my way through about fifteen similar names until I found one that struck a chord.

"Well, well, well. Along with his brother Marcel, he owns that car yard which went up in flames. Remember when we were at the funeral of your old football coach?"

"*Automobiles des Qualité?*"

"Yes."

"Who'd have thought? No wonder he'd said he had things on his mind. Get back to the agreement."

Again I did as Remy advised. "I've heard of this name here." I tapped the letter. "*Daniel Bastille.* He was bashed in the street before I went to Türkiye and subsequently died."

"Stop picking at bits and pieces of the thing. Read the whole letter from the top!"

I began to make a go of it. "*We the undersigned...*I think that's the word... *agree to form a corporation to be known as ...*" I took a breath. "*Consolidated Investment Holdings of the Cote d'Azur. (CIH-D'AZ).* That's the name I recognised in Francine's office."

"So you said. I'm not thick. Read on."

"*It is to be legally registered as a member of The Securities and Commodity and Brokerage Industry.* Legally? Doesn't that imply they were once thinking of something *illegal*?"

"Stop trying to second guess them. Read on."

I read slowly, mispronouncing the occasional word. "*Our aim is to invest in the development of projects deemed worthy by the signatories below. The principal aim is to procure property to further the advancement of the goals of CIH-D'AZ. Each signatory is to receive an equal value, to be regarded as one share.*"

"There's nothing secretive about that," said Remy.

"Seven or eight signatures follow. Holy *Merde!*"

"Stop blessing shit and read!" snapped Remy, his eyes fixed on the road ahead.

"*Albert Tarrant.* I know him. He's the chairman of the *Nicois-Messena Group* which sponsors art events on Cote d'Azur. He's listed here as key principal."

"So? There's no crime in being a key principal on a document. Next?"

"*Daniel Bastille.* Now, what did Raphael Legrande say about him? Yes! He's a gangster who's never lost the taste for implementing his own punishment." I turned to Remy. "I think this is heavy stuff, Remy."

Remy said nothing, merely nodding in agreement, beginning to think similarly.

"Also, Dr Armand said she'd treated Danny Bastille for burns at the hospital." I dropped the letter to my knees. "Raphael Legrande suspected him of torching Gunther and Marcel's used car business."

"And Gunther found out it was him and beat him to death?"

"Not to death, technically. He died of a heart attack in hospital." I was starting to join the dots again! "This could be Gunther's list of candidates for retribution."

"I bet that fire was lit to get rid of the car yard," said Remy, his thoughts totally in sync with mine, "and force the brothers to sell. What did the letter say back there about the property?"

I re-read aloud: *procure property to further the advancement of the goals of CIH-D'AZ.*

"*Procure,* is an interesting term—in this context."

"Yes, it certainly is."

"And this agreement is the real reason Gunther's desperate to get back his chess set." Remy was likewise joining the dots. "You heard Monsieur Ballant. The value of the chess set is more sentimental than monetary."

"Hunh!" I scoffed. "There's nothing sentimental about Danny Bastille's death. You're right. Gunther wants it back to keep up his revenge. I wonder what this group wanted with that car yard of his?"

Remy thought a while as he moved into the centre lane to overtake a truck travelling slower than we were.

"What's around it?" He asked.

"What do you mean?"

"What's on either side of the car yard? Check on your map app. Have a look at what buildings surround that car yard."

I took out my phone and banged in *Automobiles des Qualitié.*

"There's a vacant block next door on its left, what looks like an old disused warehouse on its right, and a public green space which wraps around all three."

"Maybe the brothers Valleaux were standing in the way of a very large property acquisition," supposed Remy. "Let's say this group has already *procured* the vacant block and the disused warehouse."

"Private property can be acquired through a financial offer or coercion, but a public park? They'd have to deal with local government to get their hands on that."

Remy scoffed. "And all those local government officials are in no way open to a financial back-hander?" Remy scoffed again, underlining his cynicism. "Read on."

"Bingo! *Maurice St Romain,* Mayor of Nice!" I didn't add: *and fiancé of Francine Delange.*

Remy's brain was on the ball. "There's your local government connection."

I feared Remy was correct. *How does this connection affect Francine? She'd been holding onto this agreement and her fiancé's signature is on it!*

"Stop daydreaming, Dougay. Continue!"

I ran my finger down the letter. "*Yves Dulac.* I've never heard of him. Do you know that name?"

"Yves Dulac? I knew a Genevieve Dulac once. I wonder whatever became of her?"

"Remy!"

"No, never heard of him."

"*Felice Dupont.* Ever heard of her?"

"No."

"There's something about that name," I commented. "*Felice*, not *Dupont*." I sat ruminating.

"Well," said Remy, growing impatient with my inaction, "look her up on the internet as well."

I tapped her name into my mobile. "Oh no," I groaned.

"What? What is it?"

"I know her. She's none other than Felicity Deschamps, the wife of ex-deputy Mayor Pierre Deschamps. She's a scheming bitch. I met her when she introduced herself as Felice Ardoin. It appears Dupont is her family name."

I hit the exit command, sending Felicity's early photo and potted biography back into the ether where it belonged. I suddenly felt a lot cleaner. Putting the mobile back into my pocket, I returned my attention to the letter. "*Guy Moreau.* Ever heard of him?"

"No. Wait on. There was a Guy Moreau who'd been a yachtsman, Olympic Games if I recall. I think he married into money—some society woman who owned half of Monaco. That type of money."

"So, no woman who'd be interested in you."

"Read on!"

"*Edward Contant.*"

"Hunh," snorted Remy.

"You know him?"

"No. However, I know the name *Contant*. I probably know this man's father, old Marcus Contant. He was a dodgy boxing promoter from the old days."

"*Delphine Dubois.* Any ideas?"

"No, never heard of her."

I read on, out loud, carefully pronouncing the words. "*We each agree to lodge by the agreed date the investment capital of 750,000 Euro.*"

"How many signatories?"

I cast my eye down the list, totalling the names. "Seven."

"Seven multiplied by seven hundred and fifty grand? That's a tidy investment sum."

"That's over five million!"

"I *can* do mental arithmetic, Dougay." I ignored him. Remy went on. "They're very serious about this company succeeding."

I took out my mobile.

"What are you doing now?"

"I'm going to take a photo of this for Francine."

"Just give her the letter."

"What? And have Gunther know we found it? And have the Valleaux brothers deal with us on some dark night like they may have dealt with Danny Bastille?"

I took a photo of the letter and carefully re-folded it down its original lines, slipping it back into the secret drawer, closing it and clutching the chess set once again to my chest with greater concern for its well-being than previously.

Chapter 21

It was dark when Remy pulled up in front of Gunther Valleaux's place. Upon hearing Remy's truck shudder to a stop, Gunther opened the front door and strode to meet us on the footpath. I guess he wasn't inviting us inside for a late-night cocoa and a thank-you biscuit. I climbed out and carefully presented him with the chess set, as if he'd won it, along with a seafood voucher, at the local football club raffle.

"I'm sorry, Gunther," I began, "sometimes my belief in my fellow human beings gets the better of me."

He said nothing, merely grunted as he snatched it back.

I moved behind the truck and peered back around, observing. Gunther couldn't wait to get inside before needing to be reassured his stolen document was safely in its hidey-hole. He pushed against the spring-loaded lock. The shallow drawer slid out. Registering the presence of the letter, he slid the drawer shut and headed indoors. I turned and climbed up onto the bench seat next to Remy. "Let's go," I quietly told him.

Remy drove away, his truck behaving itself.

"He didn't check on the state of the chess pieces, only if the letter was there."

"Clearly, it's not the jade that's irreplaceable," Remy commented, dryly.

"And we're not suspected of having laid eyes on the letter," I said, feeling relieved.

"A can of worms," said Remy. "That letter, that car yard fire, that death of Danny Bastille. Sometimes it's best not to know everything, and best not to try to connect all the dots when you don't have to." He warned, "So, no more about that fire in the car yard and that *procurement* of property."

"Of course, how could I possibly get involved with that?" I asked. "It's over, isn't it?" Though I confess, deep down I was still concerned about any trouble coming Francine's way.

"And finally, my last warning," Remy stressed. "No more Good Samaritan stuff. Forget trying to smooth the rough course of young love. Okay?"

"Okay."

Remy didn't believe me. He and I both knew I wasn't going to fundamentally change. We drove on in silence. At the top of Avenue Auber, Remy let me out. I bid him, "Goodnight. I'll be in touch."

"Please don't threaten me."

*

Early in the morning, Francine called and asked if I could come to her office sometime today.

"Are you okay?" I asked, a touch of concern audible in my question.

"Of course, why shouldn't I be?"

"It's fortuitous you called me," I said cheerily. "I have a surprise for you."

"I've seen it and it's no surprise!"

I ignored her suggestive gag. "What time? Do you feel like lunch? When I show you what I've got, you'll beg to feed me!"

"Dougay," she said, becoming serious, the lawyer to the fore, "you have to pay me some money. I need you to come to my office and sign papers. I've drawn up the contracts, company material, registrations, tax accounts and bank accounts for the company Skipper, Matty and you are involved in. *Wide Blue Sea Cruises* is now a going concern."

*

"Congratulations, Dougay, again," said Francine, extending her hand formally. We shook. "First five per cent, then another fifteen per cent in *L'Opera Mozart,* full ownership of a mini art exhibition, ownership of a luxurious apartment and now this—controlling interest in a luxury cruising company. A responsible woman could very easily fall for you. Thank goodness I'm not responsible." I let that comment pass. "So, what is it you wished to show me?"

I took out my mobile phone and found the photo of the letter in the jade chess set. I turned it slowly towards her.

"Where did you get that?" She asked, her eyes widening in disbelief. "Did you take this photograph?"

143

"Yes."

"Please hand me the letter."

"I don't have it."

"How did you come across it? It couldn't possibly have been in Türkiye!"

"No, Francine, of course, it wasn't; however, I don't think I should tell you where I stumbled upon it. Like you say to me, it's safer if you don't know everything." She sat staring at the photograph on my phone. "I'll send you this so you can have it for your files.

"Dougay," she began, leaning into me as if we may be overheard, "I need to know where that letter is. You need to tell me."

"I don't think I should. As I said, I don't want you getting hurt." I thought about that. "Or me."

"Dougay, I'll be brutally honest with you. If I don't get back the original of that letter, if people find out I've lost the only copy of that agreement, then I'll be in more serious trouble than you think you're protecting me from. I need to have it *here*."

"I don't have it."

"So how did you take this photo?"

"I'd rather not say."

"Dougay, *please*. You *have* to *help* me."

Francine had never begged me for anything. I began to nod, half-thinking aloud, "Perhaps I could get it for you."

"How much?"

"No, I don't need payment, Francine."

"I meant, how much would this *thief* want?"

"Oh, he's not interested in money." She didn't understand and I wasn't about to explain. So much for me vowing to Remy I'd go nowhere near the ongoing business of that car yard fire.

"Whatever. I'll leave it up to you to get it returned and before you do, delete that photo from your phone."

Francine came around her desk and stood over me, the black bra of hers clearly visible through her white blouse. "I can't thank you enough, Dougay," she said, placing her hand on my shoulder. "I'm sure you'll be able to get it back. I believe in you."

How was I possibly going to get back that letter of agreement? Go ask Gunther? Break into his house? *I think not! Dougay, you should have kept your mouth shut!*

Francine's receptionist called from outside, "I'm off for that appointment now, Madame Delange!"

Francine opened the door and went into the outer office.

I sat back, worrying. *How am I possibly going to get back that letter? Gunther Valleaux is no easy push-over.*

Francine locked the outer door and unbuttoned her blouse when she entered behind me. With one swipe, she cleared the top of her desk. I knew what that gesture meant!

"Francine, I don't know how I'm going get that letter back."

"You clearly need an incentive to rid yourself of your hesitancy," she said, sitting on her desk and pulling me towards her. "I need that letter."

As she began to undo my belt, I reminded myself, *you're not a thief, Dougay! You're an idiot, that's what you are, but you're not a thief.*

Francine kissed my ear. Her breath was warm. Then she started gently nibbling. "I need that letter back," she whispered, "as soon as possible."

As she ran her hand up my chest I wondered, *how am I possibly going to get the letter in the jade chess set back?*

I didn't wonder about that for long. I had another, more pressing agenda to be going on with.

*

"Francine, when you get home, draw your blinds, lock your door and don't let anyone in."

"Why?" She asked, buttoning her blouse.

"I trusted you before, now it's your turn to trust me." Another concern hit me. "How *do* you get home?"

"What is this, Dougay?" She reached for her jacket hanging on the stand off the side of her desk. "What are you going on about?"

"Francine, I'm serious. How do you get home?"

"I usually walk. Unless I have a lot of papers, then I'll phone for a taxi. Why?"

"Phone for a taxi. Until I get that letter back, I'd feel a lot better knowing that you are vigilant."

Francine buttoned her jacket and stood still as if confronting me. "Come on, Dougay. What's going on? What do you know you're not telling me?"

"Remember the time I said I'd look out for you? Well, now's the time."

"Oh, okay, okay," she replied, giving in. "Whatever you say, Monsieur Bodyguard." She stacked some papers.

I found her briefcase on the floor and passed it to her. "I'll work something out by tomorrow. You shouldn't be left alone in Nice."

"I truly don't know what you're concerned about." She put the papers into her briefcase. "Tomorrow I'll be in Monaco. Maurice has family events he and I must attend all weekend."

I breathed easier knowing that.

*

In the morning, I headed to the marina in Cannes, for Skipper, Matty and I needed to spend time together to begin serious discussions on how we were going to begin to make a success of *Wide Blue Sea Cruises*. I couldn't see anything really happening until next summer, though I knew a lot of preparation would be needed before then.

On board the train, I went over and over in my head that foolish promise I'd made to Francine.

Dougay, why do you say you'll do things which are nigh impossible? You're only going to disappoint Francine! Pulling into the station, I clicked my fingers. *There's one very, very, very slim chance.* I pondered that thought. *Wait until after the weekend, Dougay. And then only if, only if.* Yes, from out of left field I had stumbled upon a possible solution.

*

On board the *Blue Dahlia*, passing Monaco, a large luxury cruiser, strikingly coloured in black, red and grey was anchored a little further from shore than the other boats. It was one of the many floating palaces along the Cote d'Azur that people with too much money needed to acquire.

"That's one hell of a first-rate boat," I admired.

146

"Yes, makes the *Blue Dahlia* look like a row boat," assessed Matty.

"Still, she's *your* little row boat!"

He laughed and went up to the bridge to ask Skipper something. I studied the luxury cruiser. On the top deck, taking in the sun sat four people, two men and two women, drinking champagne, served by a white-jacketed waiter. After a while Matty returned.

"What did you need to know?" I asked loudly above the noise of the boat ploughing through the sea.

"I asked Skipper if he knew who owns that impressive boat."

"And?"

"An ex-Olympic gold yachtsman," said Matty, impressed. "Well, apparently it really belongs to the wife. You know, serious money that goes back a long way."

I recalled what Remy had told me on the way back from Arles. I offered the name, "Guy Moreau?"

"How'd you know that?"

*

Matty and I finished the washing up after he'd once again cooked a first-rate meal. The two of us joined Skipper up on deck. Overhead, the stars twinkled. I couldn't recall one of Big Barry's songs to go with the image. I'm sure Skipper and Matty were thankful.

"I suggest," I began, "that for all the things we know nothing about—we farm out to other agents. Like bookings," I qualified. "I've had dealings with Madame Cartier at *Eastern Mediterranean Tours* and she is very efficient, honest and reliable. Perhaps, she could become our exclusive booking agent."

Skipper suggested, "We need to have a few 'fake' runs, dress rehearsals for friends, to see in what areas we are going to be deficient."

Matty added, "I think we're going to need at least two wait-staff on board."

I suggested to Matty that he do an operating budget. I also explained to them that I saw my role as being in the background—way in the background. "I'd much prefer that you and Skipper run the show. It is after all your boat. I trust you both."

That was all they needed to hear. I passed across to them the papers I had signed at Francine's office and they added their signatures. The three of us shook hands and Matty took a selfie of the moment.

Skipper looked skyward. "I might take the boat in a little closer to shore, just in case a wind blows up during the night." Skipper kicked over the engines and we slowly headed into that bay where I'd fallen heavily for Mary-Anne Walton.

We anchored in close to shore and drank bubbly, just like Guy Moreau and those other rich people on that impressive yacht. I raised my glass and offered a toast, "To absent friends."

They raised their glasses. We drank to Mary-Anne. I sat up a little, leaning into them and asking sotto voce, "Did she have far to swim, when she stepped off the boat?"

"She didn't step off the boat," said Skipper.

"She left from the beach in a car," added Matty.

I said nothing. I visualised her on the sand, kissing them both farewell, combined tears, her walking away from the water to the waiting vehicle, climbing into the back seat and disappearing to safety.

Skipper pointed off to the right. "Italy's just over there, remember. It helped to have an Italian driver for the first stage of her disappearance."

"Do you know where she is?" I asked, checking, if, for them, her disappearance was complete. I wasn't going to tell them what I knew.

"No. The least we know the better. After all, she is dead," said Matty.

Skipper stated ironically, "We don't wish to have our inheritance taken from us."

"Nor jailed for fraud," added Matty.

No, I thought. *We do not wish that*. I pondered out loud, "An Italian driver…anyone I know?"

"Probably," said Matty, giving nothing away.

"The only Italian I know is Big Luigi," I said. "Pierre Legrande's bodyguard."

Skipper leant forward and tapped my knee, confirming my thoughts. The puzzle was complete.

Chapter 22

We made a day of it. After breakfast, we took the rubber dinghy ashore and wandered the small stony beach, lying in the sun, swimming in the deep blue water. Matty had with him a portable ice chest with enough cold chicken in it to feed an army. We swam again in the afternoon and towards 4 p.m., Skipper said that we'd better get going. We piled ourselves, along with our paraphernalia and rubbish, into the dinghy and headed back to the *Blue Dahlia.* Skipper let me steer her out of the bay, though soon near the open sea the task became too great a responsibility and I gladly let him take over once more.

As we passed Monaco, I again admired that luxury cruiser. Matty noticed my interest and handed me a pair of binoculars.

"What's the boat called?" I shouted up to Skipper on the bridge.

"*Lucky Lady-Love.*"

"That's a mouthful!"

Skipper called back, "The owner actually loves the rich woman he married."

An orange rubber dinghy sped from the landward side to the cruiser. It travelled so quickly that I thought it was going to smack into the side of the luxury boat. At the bow, it pulled up suddenly, metres short, its outboard engine howling at the dramatic change of gear.

The man operating the dinghy stood, unsteadily at first, shrugging his shoulders and twitching his head. I knew that gesture! Then maintaining his balance, he hurled something fizzing through the air onto the boat. Black hair, unshaven, powerfully built, revengeful Gunther Valleaux had recommenced working his way through the list of names on the *CIH-D'AZ* agreement.

Gunther savagely throttled the dinghy, and it roared down to the yacht's stern, spewing behind it a huge wake. There he brought it again to a dramatic screaming halt. Wasting no time, he threw another fizzing package up on board. Again he throttled the rubber dinghy and it sped away, though not towards Monaco Harbour, rather in the direction we'd come.

I heard Skipper shout and felt our boat change course. Nearing the vessel, on board we could hear panicked shouting. A man jumped overboard, followed by another. Two women hesitated, then held hands and jumped, followed by the crew and white-jacketed waiter. To his credit, the captain was last!

Behind them, as their heads came up from the water, gasping for air, two explosions rocked the sky.

Skipper held the *Blue Dahlia* as near as he dared to the burning boat. Matty readied our dinghy. I kept the binoculars on the people in the water, the flames a spectacular backdrop to their plight.

I didn't like what I saw. One woman was in trouble. The others were unaware of her, as they were swimming to save themselves, to get as far as possible from the burning boat.

As Matty climbed in the dinghy, I shouted, "I'll look after the floundering woman! Save the rest!"

Matty turned over the outboard motor. I whipped off my shirt and shorts, dived in and swam for the woman. I thrashed out the fastest seventy metres I had in me.

"It's okay," I managed to splutter. "I'll save you. Hang onto my shoulders." She clung to them. "Easy, easy! I have you."

"Look at my boat!" she screamed. "Look at my boat!"

I was pleased she was concentrating on that and not on staying afloat which meant I didn't have to fight her panicked thrashings. "I'm going to put my arms around you and swim you away. Okay?"

"Who would do such a thing? I saw a man in a rubber boat…" she spluttered, spitting water.

I lifted her onto my hip and began to side-stroke her slowly away. Twenty metres on, I was tired. "Grab around my waist from behind." She did so. I swam freestyle without kicking, the woman holding on, her chin digging into the back of my shoulders.

The others had climbed into our rubber dinghy and Matty steered it over to us. I stopped swimming. Kicking my legs furiously, I held myself upright in the water and managed to lift the woman towards Matty. He took her and one of the rescued crew helped Matty pull her into the dinghy.

"You go, Matty. I'll swim back."

I floated on my back for a while catching my breath, watching Matty steer the dinghy back to the *Blue Dahlia*.

When I got back on board, Matty had all of them wrapped in blankets and Skipper was taking a reading of the position where the boat had exploded. He radioed the information to the SNSM, the coast guard, not that they wouldn't have heard it, or seen it from shore. And of course, by now, every media outlet on the Cote d'Azur would be beginning an enquiry into it.

I didn't have to be introduced to Guy Moreau. He was the one standing, dripping water, fuming, not believing his eyes, staring at the burning shell of his million-euro cruiser. Wrapped in a towel, I stood near him looking at it, my silence comment enough.

Skipper shouted, "The fuel tanks are still to explode! Everybody down!"

Skipper was correct. The *Lucky Lady-Love* exploded again, a huge ball of gushing orange flame and billowing red fire spewing forth. Debris fell from the sky, luckily falling short of us.

Guy Moreau took out his phone from his soaking-wet designer walking shorts and took a photo! All this before he enquired how his wife was! He saw me studying him. "Insurance," he said, bitterly.

The other man came over and the three of us stood there, gathered as one by the side railing, staring at the luxury cruiser burn to the water line. The man said to Guy, "My laptop."

"You have back-ups on shore?"

"Of course."

"That's a relief," muttered Guy. "We certainly don't want the marine investigators finding..." he stopped abruptly, aware I was standing with them.

"Sir," I said to Guy Moreau, "that woman there, who I assume is your wife, is shivering, badly. Cold. Shock. I don't think it would be appropriate for *me* to put my arm around her and rub her warm."

"Yes, of course." He crossed over to her.

"What happened?" I asked the other man, deliberately not mentioning what I'd witnessed. He made no indication of having heard me. "Was there a fire in the galley?" I persisted. Again he refused an answer. There was something very cold about him and it wasn't brought on by the loss of his laptop or his dip in the ocean. He withdrew, leaving me alone by the railing.

Guy Moreau's wife was now wrapped in her husband's arms, quietly crying. She suddenly stood and spat at him, "If this has anything to do with those...those...new friends of yours!"

The 'cold' man eyed her outburst with distaste.

"Keep your voice down!" Guy Moreau spat back.

Maybe they're not so in love as everyone believes, I thought, noting their body language and the venom in her voice.

Guy's captain was up on deck with Skipper, two old sea dogs looking back, unable to believe what they'd witnessed. The three members of the crew were safely sitting on the stern with Matty drinking hot coffee, blankets wrapped around themselves, shivering. I didn't care what they did, or wore. I was just pleased no one had lost their lives.

*

No boat explodes and goes unnoticed. As Skipper headed into Monaco, Guy Moreau climbed up and had a word with him. The *Blue Dahlia* changed course and headed over towards Nice. Matty followed Guy back down onto the deck.

I whispered to Matty, "What was that about?"

"Guy Moreau doesn't want to be taken to Monaco Harbour. He doesn't want to be part of the spectator side-show or address the media pack which will be awaiting our arrival. We'll take them back to our mooring in Cannes. They'll call for cabs to take them home."

"Won't the police want to interview them all?"

"Well, being wealthy," began Matty, dropping his voice, "maybe their attitude is: *the police can come to us*."

I went below deck, found a dry towel and changed back into my clothing.

Up on deck, I observed Guy Moreau spend about twenty minutes on his mobile, making various calls, explaining, threatening, demanding—of whom I had no idea. Of one thing I was sure—it didn't sound as if he was speaking to his insurance company or calling for a taxi. I wondered how long it would take him, or his connections, to figure out Gunther Valleaux had tossed the dynamite. And when they did, what did they intend to do about it?

After the phone call, Guy and the 'cold' man held a long, private, whispered conversation. Occasionally, one would stand, take a few steps, consider something, return and they'd put their heads together again.

The two women sat holding each other, wrapped in blankets, towels over their heads, their clothing drying over a chair in the warm evening breeze. I would have dearly loved to have sat with them and learnt more; however, I knew the two men, and perhaps the women as well, would misconstrue, when all I wanted to do was eavesdrop.

As Skipper entered Cannes harbour, Guy, belatedly, after a strong reminder from his wife, phoned for a taxi.

Once Skipper had docked and Matty had secured the boat, Guy, in front of his wife and followed by the other couple, strode away down the pier. Only Guy's wife turned and waved a final 'thank you' to us. Their crew would have to find their own way home.

Thankfully, no media pack awaited us. No pack; however, one intrepid journalist stood on the pier.

I was standing on the stern of the boat giving the rescued crew some euros so they could take a train home to wherever they lived when I heard an excited voice call, "Dougay! Dougay Roberre!" It belonged to ace reporter, Mimi Benoit.

Just the time I'd like anonymity, she remembers my name! I waved. "Mimi! Give me a moment!"

Matty and I saw the crew off. I bid Skipper and Matty *au revoir* and thanked them for a most 'interesting' weekend.

"It's certainly an eventful life being associated with you, Dougay," Matty said. Skipper endorsed his comment with an ironic laugh.

Catching up with Mimi, I said, "I'd have thought you'd want to interview the rescued captain."

"Anyone can do that. What's the background?"

"Background?"

"Yes, how'd the explosion come about?"

"I wasn't on board that boat. I was on board the *Blue Dahlia*."

"Oh! I'd assumed you were working on board the exploded boat." Then she thought of what I'd said and looked again at the boat I'd just stepped off. "This is the boat owned by Harold Kempenski."

I needed to distance myself from the legacy of Kempenski and the inquisitive mind of Mimi. "No, Kempenski only leased it. The skipper, Guillaume Delanche, and first mate, Matthew Dodds, own the boat. Mimi, let's talk in a bar up in the Old Town."

*

"I'll have a white wine, Dougay," Mimi said upon entering.

I ordered two.

"Do you realise who has been rescued?" Mimi asked, not wasting time on social pleasantries. "Do you realise who owns that luxury yacht?"

I eased her from the bar to a table in the corner where we could chat privately.

"He introduced himself," I lied. "Guy someone."

"Guy Moreau, ex-Olympic sailing champion."

I raised my eyebrows and pursed my lips. "Olympic *sailing* champion?"

"Yes, the irony is not lost on me either. Did he say anything?"

"Yes—*merci.*"

"About the explosion!"

"No, nothing."

"How'd the *Blue Dahlia* rescue them?"

"We just happened to be sailing by. I helped in the rescue, though Matty is the hero. He had that rubber dinghy into the water in a flash. No, Mimi, don't write about that. If you're planning on mentioning me in your article then I'm heading home right now." She seemed to accept that; however, before she could really decide, I changed tack. "Why? Why are you not interested in this explosion?"

"Oh, I am. But another journalist, still stuck in Monaco, will get all those *official* details. I'm more interested in *why* it happened, rather than *what* happened. I repeat the question. Did Guy Moreau say anything? To you? Even in passing?"

I shook my head.

Mimi considered whether she'd tell me anything else or not. She decided she would. Looking first around the bar, checking if we were being overheard, she leant into me. "Guy Moreau is more than a married wealthy playboy sailor. He's a *businessman.*" She'd deliberately coloured the term.

"You'd better explain yourself, Mimi."

"It's only hearsay, no evidence, but it's thought he may be connected in unsavoury ways with some shady characters along the Cote d'Azur." She didn't elaborate, instead, she offered, "Buy me another drink and I'll let you know a few things I can't quite link together."

I bought us both another.

"You see there's never been a boat explosion like that, here on the Cote d'Azur for a *very, very long time.* Two or three weeks ago, there was a fire in a car yard. There's never been one of those here on the Cote d'Azur for a *very, very long time* either."

"You think they're connected?"

"A man was found beaten up and subsequently died in hospital. This dead man had burnt hands and singed eyebrows! A nurse, a contact of mine, said his hands reeked of petrol."

"Ah," I nodded, "and that hasn't happened for a *very, very long time* on the Cote d'Azur."

We smiled, both recognising our senses of humour and made a small 'toast' in appreciation of the other.

"And let me add, they were not singed from an over-active barbeque!" She took a sip of her wine. "The burn victim was a 'colourful' businessman with, I'm told by reliable sources, a violent streak. His name was Danny Bastille. Ever heard of him?"

"Danny Bastille? No," I lied.

"Two unexplained fires! Arson the cause of the first and…how did the boat explode?"

"How would I know?" I asked, impersonating Monsieur Innocent.

"You didn't see it go up? You arrived after the explosion?"

I avoided directly answering her questions. I leant in and whispered, "Sometimes you know far too much detail, Mimi." She seemed to be happy that she did.

"Dougay, I'll let you in on this. It hasn't been officially announced yet, but there's this road-works depot out of Monaco over near the Italian border, outside a pretty town called Menton. They're finally clearing a back road after a landslide eighteen months ago."

"Things move fast here on the Riviera."

She ignored my jibe. "Dynamite was stolen from this depot two nights ago."

"And you think this dynamite was used to blow up Guy Moreau's boat? Why?"

"That's what I want to find out. A used car yard fire; a dead gangster; an exploded luxury yacht and stolen dynamite. Is this the beginning of a gang war?" She paused. "We haven't had one of those on the Cote d'Azur for a *very, very long time.*"

"Guy Moreau isn't a gangster, is he?"

"I didn't say that! About Guy, it's only rumour and speculation, though not about Danny. It would be very beneficial to have a link between Danny Bastille and Guy Moreau to clarify my thinking. It could, one day, make for an explosive exposé."

A link between Danny Bastille and Guy Moreau? I sure knew where there was one—*CIH-D'AZ! Maybe there's more dynamite at hand, other than what Gunther tossed onto Lucky Lady-Love!*

Mimi went on. "Guy would have a lot of money, courtesy of his wife, to invest in all sorts of business opportunities. Maybe Guy's offended someone, double-dealed someone, stepped on someone's toes, ripped off someone. Who can say?"

"Not me, Mimi. I'm the truly ignorant one here."

"Do you know a man called Yves Dulac?"

That rings a bell, I thought. *Yes, his name is also on that letter!* "No," I said shaking my head.

"He was the other man you rescued."

The man who'd lost his laptop!

"Did you hear him say anything to Guy Moreau?"

"No, nothing, Mimi."

"Thanks for the wine, Dougay, I owe you."

"*Au revoir*, Mimi, keep your head down."

Chapter 23

"No, he's not in there," Louise said, coming out of the hostel. "Guy Franc hasn't been seen for a while. Maybe he's left town."

I had feared that crazy idea of mine had every possibility of not happening, that Guy still being in occasional residence at the hostel was simply too good to be true. Now I had to think of another way. "Come on, Louise, thanks for that. Let's go home." On the way a thought hit me. I phoned Remy. "Do you still have that number I sent you for Guy Franc?"

"Of course."

"I'd like you to call Madame Electro and see if she can locate him again."

"What's he stolen this time?"

"Nothing, I just wish to catch up—for old time's sake."

*

It was nearly an hour, waiting in the early evening light outside a nondescript apartment block, eyes fixed on the security door before I began to feel as if this too was a wasted long shot. I was seriously considering leaving and having to think up a third way of tracking them down when suddenly I heard a click from inside and quickly stepped back before the door was opened. I counted to three and stepped back around the corner. "Hi, Guys!" I called with an overly friendly tone in my voice. "What's new?"

Guy Franc took one look at me, turned and bolted—straight into the outstretched arms of Remy!

"You bastard," shouted Simone, coming for me again, her claws to the fore.

I grabbed onto her arms before they did me any further facial damage. "Settle, Simone. Or Cecily. Or whoever you are this week. Settle down. It's not what you think."

Remy and I bundled the two together, and I spoke softly to them. "I have a job for you." They didn't believe me. "For money!" They still didn't believe me. "It's true. I need you to break into Gunther Valleaux's place and steal the jade chess set."

Simone snorted. Guy scoffed, "Is this a joke?" To their credit, they didn't protest or struggle to get away.

"The same chess set?" Simone asked, obviously the brains of the outfit.

"Ironically, yes."

"How much?" Guy asked, obviously the treasurer.

"Enough to make it worth your while." They thought about that.

"A hundred," stated Simone.

"Each," added Guy.

"You two drive a hard bargain." Simone took a dramatic step away from me. "Okay. It's a deal; however, you're not to leave any damage. We must respect Gunther's property."

"No damage," said Simone. "I still have my copy of his front door key."

"That's reassuring," I said, relieved there'd be no damaged lock on Gunther's door.

Simone thought a moment. "We'll do it Tuesday evening."

"Why Tuesday?" Remy asked.

"Gunther regularly goes off to play poker with his brother and his pals."

"What if he changes his mind?"

"He won't. He's addicted to his Tuesday night ritual. He even went out to play poker the week his wife died."

"Okay. Remy will pick up both of you in his truck."

*

"I'm back in Nice," Francine informed me over the phone. "All safe and sound. No one followed me, no one threatened me, no one assaulted me. So, Monsieur Bodyguard, what do you have in mind for this evening?"

I ordered a large pizza and rang Francine's doorbell. "Ta-da!" I exclaimed, presenting her with the warm cardboard carton.

"Pizza!"

"I hope you have a few cold beers in the fridge?" I asked.

"I certainly do. Come on in. I think you know the way."

We must have both been hungry because once the beers were cracked and the pizza slices divided into two plates, we didn't say another word until after I'd washed and wiped the two plates and rinsed the beer glasses.

"How were Maurice's family gatherings?"

"Dull, dull, dull."

I put away the plates, cutlery and glasses. Francine stowed the dead pizza carton in her rubbish can. She then set about making up for her dull, dull, dull weekend with events which were exciting, exciting, exciting. For starters, she slowly let out her jet-black hair and shook it side to side as if in slow motion.

On the way out of her apartment, I said, "Lock your door and don't talk to strangers." After all, to check on her safety was the only reason I'd gone over there!

*

On Tuesday evening, under the cover of darkness, Remy's truck pulled up around the corner from Gunther's place. He killed the headlights.

"Why've you stopped here?" I asked.

Remy looked to me across Simone being nursed on Guy's knee.

"In case the truck is recognised. Remember, that's how Gunther found you in the first place!"

The four of us climbed down. I whispered to Remy. "Hadn't you better stay here by your truck?"

"If things go wrong, you're going to need me to fight off Gunther. He's too violent for you. You can't deal with him by yourself."

We walked around the corner. There was a light inside the house. We stood there a while observing. No shadow passed across it.

Remy, Guy and I held back in the shadows as Simone walked brazenly to the front door and put in the key.

I reminded Guy, "Only the jade chess set. Don't take anything else. We're not thieves!"

"Not thieves?" He queried.

"Go on, Simone's got the door open."

Guy walked passed her and entered the dimly lit house. I crossed over and waited a little away from the front door. Simone joined me.

Across the street, a house's outdoor light turned on, illuminating Remy from behind. I gestured for him to move away. Remy turned around and looked at the light as if drawn to it. I laughed to myself. *Sometimes you just can't find quality help, can you?*

Guy returned with the chess set under his arm and handed it to me.

"Guy and Simone, look away for thirty seconds. You are not to be witnesses." They looked curiously at each other and said nothing, doing as I asked.

I tapped around the base of the chess set until the secret drawer slid out. The letter was inside. I removed it, opened it to verify it was *CIH-D'AZ*, pocketed it and slid the drawer shut. "*Merci*," I said to both of them. "You can turn around now." I handed Guy the chess set. "Now return it."

"What?"

"Return it. Put it back where it belongs. I'm no thief."

Chapter 24

The next morning ushered in more than just bright sunshine. I was over outside Francine's office, leaning against the door when she emerged from the elevator.

"Bright and early as you asked for, Dougay. What's the surprise?"

"I'll show you inside."

Francine unlocked her office and turned on the lights.

"Your secretary isn't in today?"

"No, today she's at a bookkeeping course. So what do you have for me?"

I held the *CIH-D'AZ* letter under my chin while Francine clapped her hands in delight.

"You're my hero!"

Before I could drop it, she kissed me. As we separated, she took the letter and promptly returned it to her filing cabinet. She locked it and then checked she'd done so, taking no chances.

"What are you doing Friday evening, late? I have to be at an early evening reception with colleagues; however, I should be home after ten, ten-thirty. Oh wait…that's the following Friday. This Friday…I…no, I can't. Sorry. You understand, don't you, Dougay?"

*

I left Francine's office and drifted down the stairs, pleased with myself. I even whistled a ditty on the lower step. *Another successful adventure, Dougay!* I pushed open the front door and began to walk off. From behind, I heard sudden footsteps and a shadow on the building to my left moved rapidly. I ducked.

A loud clunk hit the wall above my head. Before I could fully turn and confront my attacker, the handle of a baseball bat was savagely stabbed into my solar plexus.

"Phoar!" I fell forward from the waist.

The baseball bat was raised and I turned a little, managing to tuck my arm into my side. The bat smashed into it. Though I'd protected myself, I felt the blow right into my rib cage. I fell to the footpath.

"Idiot! Dumb assed idiot! You came to steal the letter with your old mate, the ex-fighter, Remy Didion." Gunther Valleaux smacked the baseball bat down onto my upper arm. "A neighbour recognised him. Dumb assed idiot!"

I knew a kick would be coming next, so fighting my body pain, I lifted my legs up into my midriff and made myself into the tightest ball possible. I was right. The kick came. And so did the next explosion of pain.

I heard a car pull up near me. Doors opened and feet ran. I squinted looking up into the sunlight. A man hit Gunther from behind. A second man smothered his face with a cloth. Gunther struggled. The first man jabbed him in the kidneys as fiercely as he could. The second man held the cloth there until Gunther began to go limp. The two men bundled him into the car.

A third man bent over me. He firmly placed his hand on the back of my head and held my face to the pavement, squashing my cheek. "Keep your eyes down. For your own safety, keep them there for a count of thirty after the car drives away. Forget everything you think you witnessed here today."

With my head pushed into the pavement, I saw a tattooed hand, a snake entwining a dagger, take hold of Gunther's red aluminium baseball bat.

The voice muttered, "Might be useful one day."

*

I didn't want Francine to know what had happened so I stumbled my way to a corner cafe and ordered a double whiskey. Not terribly French, I know, but I needed to ease the pain, and I'm not a fan of Absinthe or Pernod or anything of that nature. The waiter looked at me, looked at the clock on the wall and didn't comment any further. I sat gingerly outside in the sliver of sunlight and knocked it back. Swallowing hurt. Before the barman returned inside, I called out, "I'll have another."

My mobile rang. It was Francine. "Sorry, Dougay, something's come up. Can you come back here within the hour?"

"Your office?" I asked as the whiskey began to hit my head.

"Yes. I may need protection after all. I need you to sit in the front office, perusing a contract, uninterested in whatever takes place. Just in case, though I don't expect, and certainly hope there won't be physical trouble."

"Francine, I'll come over now." I went inside the cafe, paid the barman for both whiskeys and skulled the second as I'd done the first. After my two doses of 'medicine', I felt a whole lot better, the blows from the baseball bat beginning to ease.

*

Sitting as a client in Francine's outer office, I perused the contract she'd handed me. It was my sixth time through the document, which with my limited French was not making any more sense than it had the first time.

To my left, the outer door tentatively opened. I kept 'reading', my head down uninterested in whoever walked in. Patent leather shoes beneath a grey tailored suit crossed to Francine's door. The man knocked.

Francine opened her door, ushering him inside. She left the door ajar, so I could hear. It didn't register with the man that she had, for he had other things on his mind.

"Madame Delange," he began formally, "the letter of agreement—*CIH-D'AZ*—do you still have it?"

"Yes. Why wouldn't I?"

"I'd like to see it, please," he said without friendliness.

Francine crossed to her filing cabinet, unlocked it, flicked through and handed a file to the man. He studied it for a moment. He handed it back to her. "Thank you, Francine. I hope you've been well."

"Very well. Is there a reason for wishing to see the letter?"

"A fellow signatory was concerned for its whereabouts."

I reasoned *they'd learnt from a tortured Gunther about the stolen letter from Francine's office.*

"Why would it not be here?" An offended Francine asked.

The man didn't answer that, instead, he said, "This fellow signatory is all for sending you a warning, a warning to maintain security and to ensure attorney-client confidentiality."

"Don't I always?"

Silence returned; the man must have been reading. Eventually, he said, "It's all in order. Francine, I'm pleased the letter is here. Its presence is reassuring, though at the same time very puzzling. Some of my fellow signatories feel someone had a list of our names and was exacting revenge."

Had? Was? Past tense! Is Gunther dead?

"What do you mean?" Francine asked.

"I can say nothing further. *Au revoir*, Francine." The man turned to go, though stopped in the doorway and turned back to her. "You're looking more beautiful by the day. How many years has it been we've known each other?"

Francine didn't reply. She escorted the man out of her office, past me and into the corridor outside.

I knew the man. I'd been introduced to him by Madame Legrande at a society art auction. He was Albert Tarrant, chairman of the *Nicois-Messena Group* and principal signatory of *CIH-D'AZ!*

*

I turned on my computer before going to bed. There was a chatty email from international swimsuit model Sue-Lin Cambridge, with another photo attachment. I clicked on it. *This woman has been blessed with too much beauty!* Not the type of beauty you want to get all aroused over and smother in kisses and start your heart beating in double time, but rather the type you want to stand back and admire in awed silence.

Studying her photograph, I thought about that a little longer. No, I was wrong. Her beauty brought forth both desires in me.

One day I'm going to have to ask her to stop being so friendly towards me, telling me her secret thoughts, her dreams for the future, her thinking I was her best friend. We'd only met once! Even so, I'd become her electronic pen pal over these past few months. I'm going to have to write her an email in which I'll explain to her the sort of man I really am. I hope it won't come as too much of a shock to her, for I'm sure she thinks I'm noble, honourable and heroic. I fear she reads too much romantic fiction.

I downloaded the photograph, dominated by her naked back, her head turning towards the camera's lens delivering the most beguiling smile I think I've ever seen. Am I impressed by such female beauty? I sure am. I made the photograph my screensaver!

My mobile rang. "I think you'd better come back here." It was Francine and she was very concerned about something.

"Are you okay?" I asked sitting up in bed.

"Yes, yes, I'm not hurt. It's just I think I'm going to need your assistance."

The time on my phone read: *21.24.*

"Are you home?" I asked getting up.

"No, I'm at the office."

"You're working late."

"Yes. Bring your swimming trunks."

Chapter 25

The door to Francine's office was ajar. I didn't like that. I carefully eased it open. There was no need for concern. Inside, Francine was alone, leaning on her secretary's desk, facing me with pink washing-up gloves on her hands.

"Are you cleaning?"

"No." She stepped away from the desk and revealed a medium-sized cardboard box. Before I could cross to her she said, "Use these." She rolled off the rubber gloves and handed them over. I tugged them over my larger hands, eased back a flap of the lid of the cardboard box, and recoiled.

"Yes," she said, "it's not a pretty sight, is it."

I took a closer look. The object was wrapped in clear cling plastic wrap, the type you cover food, when keeping it fresh in a refrigerator. The wrapped object was a man's hand, a man's left hand, a man's left hand with a pirate ring—skull and crossbones worn on the fourth finger.

"Gunther Valleaux," I muttered.

"You know who it belongs to?" Francine asked with surprise and concern.

"Yes. Gunther is the man who stole the *CIH-D'AZ* letter from your filing cabinet."

"He won't be wanting the letter now," muttered Francine.

"I gather you want me to get rid of this."

"No, Dougay, I thought I might ask you to mount it so I could hang it on the wall above my desk."

We both looked at each other, our sudden bursts of laughter breaking the tension in the room.

"Who Francine? Who could possibly send you this?"

"I know and I don't know. It's only a warning, Dougay. You heard Albert Tarrant."

"Albert Tarrant seems to be such a mild, well-mannered gentleman."

"No, not him, specifically. Others he's associated with would have sent it. Albert's a teddy bear. He wouldn't know anything about this."

"Have you touched it? The plastic wrapping I mean?"

"No. I know enough about DNA and fingerprints to be exceedingly careful. I need you to dispose of it."

"Where? Not simply dispose of it in the garbage in the laneway out back?"

"No. I want you to swim it out into the Mediterranean and push it towards Africa."

*

Francine carried an upmarket shopping bag, with Gunther's left hand inside, covered by a beach towel. It was now well past midnight. Even so, the lights of Nice were still bouncing across the sea. To stay in the dark as much as possible, we walked the beach beneath *Parc de la Colline du Chateau*, the high hill at the eastern end of the bay. I was thankful the restaurant on the cliff face had closed for the night because we didn't need an audience of diners peering down on us. Walking carefully across the stoney beach, our arms were wrapped around each other as if we were two lovers out for a late-night stroll after blowing all our money at *Galleries Lafayette*.

Francine stopped and looked about. "We're concealed here, Dougay. This looks like a good spot to launch yourself into the water."

"It's called *diving*, Francine." I removed my shoes and socks, dropped my jeans, and took off my shirt. It was cool standing in the night air clad only in swimming trunks.

Francine took the pink rubber gloves out of the shopping bag, put them on, and carefully withdrew Gunther's hand.

"I'm going to have difficulty swimming and holding that thing at the same time."

Francine reached forward and opened the top of my swimming trunks.

"What are you doing, Francine?"

"Put his hand down your trunks and then you'll have both hands free to swim." Without waiting for an agreement, she pushed in Gunther's hand.

"Ow!" I exclaimed in a whisper. "His ring has snagged a vital organ!"

"Sorry." Francine adjusted Gunther's grip.

"I never had a man's hand down my front before," I explained. "Does this now mean I'm gay?"

"Silly boy. At best, you're now bi-sexual." She laughed! I'm glad she did because I sure didn't.

I waddled to the water, trying to maintain balance on the rocky beach with the hand's dead weight in front dragging me forward.

"Do you know, Dougay, you're now very appealing to a certain type of woman?" I ignored her attempt at humour. "Wait!" she whispered. "You have to wear the gloves. When you take the hand out, you don't want to leave *your* fingerprints on the cling plastic."

I put on Francine's washing-up gloves, waddled five steps, arms wide, pink-covered hands flapping, maintaining balance like a demented flamingo, and slid into the water. It was cold, so I swam fiercely to warm myself. The force of my forward thrust meant Gunther's hand gripped my genitalia tighter. Tonight was proving to be a rare collection of unique experiences.

I eased off, and finding a relaxed rhythm swam for about a hundred and fifty metres. I looked about to see that I wasn't in a slipstream of light from shore. I wasn't. I pulled at the top of my swimming trunks and carefully tried to ease out Gunther's left hand. It had lodged itself down there.

"Come on, Gunther, time to let go," I whispered. His hand must have heard me. I slid it out and pushed it down under the water, thrusting it forward in the direction of Africa. "*Au revoir*, mate," I said in a funereal tone.

His hand bobbed to the surface in front of my eyes!

"Don't you want to leave me, Gunther?"

I pushed it down and it bobbed back up again!

"Get lost! Piss off!" I savagely ordered.

The plastic! There's air inside the cling wrap. What are you going to do, Dougay?

Then one of those reliable ideas I get from out of left field hit me. *Drag the plastic back and forth over the sharp edge of the skull and crossbones.* I took hold of Gunther's hand. It slipped away. I was unable to easily grip it because of the wet gloves I was wearing!

"Come here," I muttered to the hand. Kicking my legs and treading water, I squeezed it tightly as if giving it a farewell shake and managed to rub some of the cling plastic over the ring. Finally, the hand took on water. It now wanted to sink. I let it.

I swam back to Francine. "Take me home, Francine. I'm going to need a hot shower."

"Good," she said. "I'm not interested in rewarding you with a cold one."

*

They never did find Gunther Valleaux. Someone was quoted in the paper as saying he couldn't cope with the loss of his wife. Another said he never got over the fire at his used car yard. His brother hinted that the economic shock was too much for his sensitive brother to cope with. Were they talking about the same Gunther Valleaux that I'd come across?

At the end of the week, I crossed from the elevator heading out to *L'Opera Mozart*. M'sieur Pom glanced up from his desk. "That car yard owner has had a successful outcome."

I knew he wasn't talking about Gunther. "Which one?" I asked in all innocence.

"Marcel Valleaux. He's sold his fire-damaged car yard." M'sieur Pom glanced back down at his newspaper and read the quote: *I accepted an offer I couldn't refuse.*

*

On Sunday morning, Pierre Legrande found me sitting with his mother in Place Mozart. He kissed her on both cheeks and hugged her. He ignored me, as he sat beside her. I leant across her and asked him, "Where's *my* kiss?"

"I'm unable to tell you," he began to innocently explain, before sticking in the dagger. "My mother has never allowed me to utter profanities in her presence."

"You boys," said Madame Legrande, "always bickering."

"*Maman*," said Pierre, sounding alarmed, "he's Dougay. He's not my brother."

"At times, I think he could be." She smiled at me. "He needs mothering. He's such a helpless open book."

"Helpless? An open book? Dougay Roberre is the most devious, guarded, womanising immigrant France has ever let into her bosom."

169

"Yes, dear, whatever you say." She patted my knee. "Dougay listens to every tale I tell him. Remember, he went to Türkiye because *I* suggested it."

"*Maman!*" warned Pierre.

"Yes, Pierre, I know it was *your* idea, but *I* planted that idea in Dougay's head, and he had the most wonderful time."

Pierre stood. "Come on, *Maman*, I'll walk you home. You've said enough already." He took his mother by the arm and walked across Place Mozart to our apartment building. Big Luigi stayed and kept an eye on me.

The late warm summer sun was working its magic. I stretched out my legs, tilted back my head and waited for Pierre to return. A car came up from the car park below. I watched the top of it disappear down Rue Rossini. I saw old Monsieur Degas come from around a corner and head into our apartment building. A woman walked her dog across the park. Life was returning to normal—just the way I liked it.

Pierre returned. "So," he said, sitting next to me, "a job well done." Once again, he placed an envelope on my knee. "Delivery expenses for Türkiye".

"What was on the card I gave to Mary-Anne?"

"You didn't look at it?" He asked, surprised.

"No. It was none of my business."

Pierre looked sideways at me, his eyes tightening. "Just how honest are you? Is that persona of yours real or fake?"

I ignored that. "So, what was on the card?"

"Numbers to a bank account in Switzerland and a PIN. What did you think I was doing in Zurich?" I slowly nodded, now fully understanding what had happened back then. "We can't turn our back on our dear friends, can we?" He asked, more in statement than a question. "Loyalty, these days, is so undervalued."

"Yes, it is," I agreed. "And no, we cannot turn our back on our dear friends."

He dropped his voice. "For her ongoing safety, we must never try to find Mary-Anne." Pierre patted the envelope on my knee. "Remember what I say." He stood, adding with a touch of warm finality, "*Elle est morte, mate!*"